Chela was fastening
walked over to her c
She straightened wh
her luxuriant hair.

"You have beautiful hair," he said in a ragged voice.
"I hope you never cut it."

She started to say something, but words were too
mundane for what she was experiencing. Magadan
was still drawing the brush through her hair. There
was no need for him to continue doing what he was,
but Chela didn't tell him that. She would have been
content if he never stopped his caressing gestures…

Dear Reader:

We are delighted to bring you this daring series from Silhouette.

Intrigue—*where resourceful, beautiful women flirt with danger and risk everything for irresistible, often treacherous men.*

Intrigue—*where the stories are full of heart-stopping suspense and mystery lurks around every corner.*

*You won't be able to resist **Intrigue**'s exciting mix of danger, deception…and desire.*

*Please write and let us know what you think of our selection of **Intrigue** novels. We'd like to hear from you.*

Jane Nicholls
Silhouette Books
PO Box 236
Thornton Road
Croydon
Surrey
CR9 3RU

Touch a Wild Heart

VELLA MUNN

SILHOUETTE

Intrigue

*First published in Great Britain 1996
by Silhouette Books, Eton House, 18-24 Paradise Road,
Richmond, Surrey TW9 1SR*

© Vella Munn 1984

Silhouette, Silhouette Intrigue and Colophon are
Trade Marks of Harlequin Enterprises II B.V.

ISBN 0 373 22006 5

46-9607

Made and printed in Great Britain

Chapter One

Beto Sanchez was the first to notice the lean, distant man watching the five men and one woman from under lids lowered to hold the sun at bay. "He was here yesterday," the nineteen-year-old said in a voice that tripped over his newly acquired English.

Chela Reola waited perhaps the space of three breaths before unwrapping her legs and swinging lightly to her feet. She wore tennis shoes to protect her feet from the punishment of decaying twigs littering the orchard ground, but her long, browned legs were accustomed to the elements and needed no covering on the hot July afternoon. She turned boldly in the direction of the man standing beside his big, powerfully built pickup at the edge of the orchard. He wasn't wearing clothes that belonged in an orchard. The four-wheel-drive pickup bore no government license plates or anything else that would identify him as an immigration officer.

"He isn't a foreman?" Chela asked, her easy English a contrast to that of the Mexicans' around her. "You haven't seen him in any of the other orchards?"

Beto shook his head. His denial was seconded by Edwardo Burriaga, a man who had subjected his face to the elements for so many years that his age was known only to himself. "He asked questions yesterday. In Spanish. He wanted to know who the best workers were, if there were any children in the orchard. But I think he was asking other questions inside."

Chela stiffened, instantly alert. The questions the man asked raised even more questions about him. Even from here she could see that he was an Anglo. Whites coming to the orchards could only mean trouble. He couldn't be from the schools, since it was summer and the authorities were no longer concerned with truant children. But if he was asking about the best workers, he might be looking to lure some of the men and women working for Rogue Orchards to another job, one that paid no more but promised much more than it delivered. Jackson County in southern Oregon had been famous for its pear crop since before the turn of the century. In their attempts to keep up with competition, the orchardists vied with each other for the most productive work force.

"Nuez is illegal," Beto continued. "But he isn't working here today."

Chela nodded. She was so much a part of the migrants that there was no question of whether she would turn in an illegal. "Not all Anglos work for immigration," she said softly.

"Maybe he wants a woman."

The slim woman who proudly carried the heritage of the mother she barely remembered placed her hands on her hips and returned the man's bold stare. He was too far away for her to make out his features in the heavy shadows cast by the pear trees. All her ebony eyes knew for sure was that he was in superb physical condition, of average height, with hair cut by a barber and not styled by a hairdresser. She both resented and admired his direct gaze. He wanted something, and that Chela didn't like, but at least he was open about his presence. Either he would approach the small group or get back into his truck.

That was his problem. Chela had only a half hour before the sprinklers had to be reset, putting an end to the workers' English lesson. After that, she would jump into her own Jeep and drive to one of the barrios, the migrant housing, where a dozen children waited for the writing class she was giving on her own time. "If he wants a woman, he shouldn't be here," she said disdainfully and turned her back on the interruption. "There aren't any women in the orchards."

"Except you," Beto pointed out, dropping back into Spanish as he wrestled with a complex thought. "You carry yourself like a young horse. You don't eat frejoles and tortillas and get fat. Maybe it's you he wants."

Never! Chela Reola had had twenty-seven years to learn what local men thought of migrants, of anyone whose skin was darker than theirs. Although she was an American citizen with an American father, she'd long ago made her alliance with her mother's people. She had reasons no one knew of for distrusting and even hating bold-eyed men who thought all they needed was money to get their way. "He'll have to have me dead," she breathed before returning her attention to the day's lesson. The stranger was of no interest to her. Ignoring him should make that clear.

Being ignored didn't concern the man. He continued his penetrating surveillance for another five minutes, content to watch without being watched in return. He was sweating down the middle of his back and along his forehead under thick coarse hair the color of a grizzly bear, but physical discomfort was something he'd become accustomed to years ago. He was fully aware that the five men and the woman had seen him, but he'd never intended his presence to be a secret. Soon he'd approach the woman, start the relationship that was essential for his purpose. The last thing he wanted was to take her completely by surprise. It would ruin everything. As he continued to watch the slender, athletic figure among the men, he admitted that the county sheriff had been right. Chela Reola didn't come out of any mold.

Now that he'd seen her, he understood what Sheriff Duff had been getting at the other day. "She won't be what you expect," Kenneth had said when the two men were meeting in the sheriff's office. "She's a migrant teacher, but she's about as far from the teacher stereotype as you'll ever get. Besides, this is summer. She's on her own now, not working for anyone but herself. Getting close to her won't be easy. She's kind of a wild animal in a lot of ways is the best I can put it. She isn't going to bolt and run, but she isn't going to trust you either."

Joe Magadan would have to be content with that explanation. Kenneth Duff didn't have time for a more detailed description, and other things the two men had to discuss that day were more important. "I'll work out something," Magadan said as the sheriff was seeing him out. "She's a woman. I've had more than a little experience with women in my life. She'll understand how important it is for her to work with me. I can bring her around."

"But you're not going to tell her everything," Kenneth pointed out. "What happens when she puts two and two together on her own? Magadan, she's no one's fool. She'll bolt for sure then, if she doesn't tear your eyes out first. If you want my advice, move slowly and lay all your cards on the table."

Unfortunately that was the last thing Magadan could do. Grunting, the big man pushed his frame away from the pear tree he'd been resting against and ran a broad, leathery hand across his eyes. He couldn't see much of her face, but if it matched her frame— No. That wasn't part of the plan. No one, as far as he'd been able to determine, knew much of anything about Chela Reola. She'd been a migrant teacher with the district for four years, but no one knew what she'd done before that, who her friends were, if she had any family, what she did with herself when she wasn't going to schools throughout the district helping to mainstream children who had never spoken English before their parents acquired green cards and came to the United States from Mexico to work.

At least now Magadan knew a little more about how she spent her summer months. She was in a pear orchard with the workers, teaching English to teenagers who would probably never finish high school, old men who no longer dreamed of anything better, and others who faded into the shadows when an Anglo ap-

proached because they were here illegally. Those men
and their families trusted Chela Reola. Somehow he
had to find a way to get her to trust him.

The ebony-eyed woman with glistening black hair
pushed behind her ears was his link with a man who
belonged in prison. "It has to work, Chela," he
whispered into the wind. "Somehow I have to make
you understand."

Chela was again thinking about the strange, silent man
when her students hurried off to change the miles of
water pipe that were essential to the growth of the
valley's pear orchards. She was used to seeing white
men in the orchards, but they were usually foremen or
others like immigration officers whose purpose was
quickly determined. The immigration officers came at
night during sudden raids that left the orchardists
shorthanded. She had never been able to understand
that. No one except migrant workers would do the jobs
the orchardists needed done, and yet it was nearly impossible for most Mexicans to obtain the green card
they needed to stay here legally. Deporting captured
illegals accomplished nothing. They would only return.
Whatever the man's purpose, it had to have something
to do with migrants and orchards. An Anglo had no
other reason for being here.

He might be a coyote, but instinct put that possibility
at the bottom of the list. Coyotes were usually Mexicans. The Anglos in the business of smuggling illegals
were furtive men, quick moving and nervous. This
man carried himself like someone who knew who he
was and wouldn't back down from any challenge; he

simply didn't strike her as a man who made his living in the dark of night. What did she care what he did for a living? He was gone.

Chela trotted down the deeply shadowed, rutted road that cut a single path through the dense orchard until she reached her Jeep. She swung a long leg up, grabbed the steering wheel with both hands, and lowered herself onto the sun-faded seat. As she reached for the keys in her pocket, her left hand made the automatic gesture designed to push the thick mane of hair out of her eyes. She could wear her hair like most women, cut and curl it, but she was proud of its rich black length. Her hair was one of the things her mother had given her—along with skin that looked tanned in the middle of a fog-bound winter.

Before her heart had time to settle on thoughts of her mother, Chela pumped her Jeep into life and bucked it to the end of the rutted road until she reached the highway. She waited for a break in the traffic and then pulled out. As the Jeep picked up speed, she lifted her head, letting the hot wind blow her hair away from her face, drying her wet scalp. Chela had spent most of her life in the orchards, and yet she didn't know how the workers stood working there when the temperatures passed one hundred degrees and humidity from the moist ground rose to sap a man's strength.

Chela was looking forward to reaching the sterile row of unpainted cabins where the children waited. It wouldn't be any cooler there, but she'd draw her students around her in the shade of a tree, and one of the mothers would bring them water while she concentrated on the English nouns and verbs that paved the way to understanding and allowed her students to compete with their classmates when September rolled around. Maybe, if the women weren't busy with babies and meals, one or two of them would join her class.

Chela had learned that it was the women who were the most reluctant to speak English. It wasn't that they were shy around her or unsure of their ability to learn, but most migrant women thought of themselves as Mexicans. Their men might have to work here to earn a decent living, and the law might say their children had to attend American schools, but in the women's hearts the dream remained: Someday they would return to Mexico; they didn't have to learn English.

Chela knew they were wrong. True, they might someday return home, but they were in the United States now. They were not only forcing themselves to live in isolation but were placing a barrier between themselves and their school-aged children.

If just one woman sat down in the shade with Chela and the children and learned how to ask for milk and eggs in a grocery store, her day would be a success. And if only children surrounded her—at least Chela had the evening to look forward to. Her soccer team had a game scheduled for five thirty in the city park.

A rare smile touched her face. It parted her soft lips and revealed perfect white teeth. How she'd become labeled an expert at soccer she didn't know. It certainly wasn't because she could execute a dribbling feint or jackknife her body in midair to produce the body swing needed to head a ball. But Chela could translate the words of a coach into words a team of Mexican boys

understood. At first she was reluctant to offer her services to the parks and recreation department because
the department's soccer program hadn't been set up to
accommodate a team consisting of Mexican players,
but this year there was a college student working as a
coach who didn't care what language his players spoke
as long as they were enthusiastic.

Jeff Cline knew a little Spanish but not enough to get
the team through practice and games without confusing
everyone. That was where Chela came in. When the
head of the parks and recreation department intro-
duced her to the man in his early twenties, Chela found
herself responding positively. Soccer was a sport most
Mexican boys already knew how to play. Why not give
them the opportunity to play under organized conditions complete with sponsors who bought their uniforms?

After her lesson at the barrios, she went home to
shower and change into the blue-and-white shirt with
lettering on the back that identified her as one of the
coaches. She thought briefly about eating, but the day
had been so hot that all she wanted was iced tea. The
game would be over around dark; maybe she'd feel like
eating then. Half of the team was already at the city-
owned park by the time Chela showed up.

"These kids are really pumped. They have twice my
confidence," Jeff told her as she joined the young
coach on the sidelines. "I just hope they can handle a
loss."

Chela placed her hands on her hips and stretched her
neck backward in order to ease a kink in her spine. The
movement elongated her slender neck and accented

the strong lines of her jaw. It also caused her firm breasts to push against the fabric of her uniform. What there was of her stomach sunk between her hipbones and was lost. As the sound of chattering boys settled around her, Chela felt her body relax. This was where she wanted to be, what she wanted to be doing.

"They aren't going to lose," she said confidently. "These kids were playing soccer from the time they could walk. Of course, they didn't have real balls or grassy fields, but they have the skills. I just wish we could get the newspaper to come out and take some pictures."

"We can't even get these characters to sit still long enough for me to talk to them, let alone pose for pictures." Jeff bent over to tie his shoes. "Jose's beside himself. I guess his dad got off work early to come to the game. The whole family's here."

Chela nodded. Jose was one of the best players on the team, a fourteen-year-old who could probably pass for seventeen. She'd already had one talk with Jose's father about how important it was that the boy stay in school next year instead of dropping out and going to work. True, with seven young boys and girls, Jose's family needed all the money they could get to support the family. Jose felt that pressure. But he was quick to learn, with an easy familiarity around science that would lead him out of the orchards if only he could get the formal education he needed. Chela hoped to have time to ask Jeff to talk to Jose after the game. The intense teenager looked up to the college student. He'd listen to Jeff when he wouldn't listen to a woman. Chela might find fault with the traditional Mexican view of women having more worth as mothers and cooks than the givers of wisdom, but she understood that tradition and looked for ways of making an impression despite it.

That was another reason she had agreed to work with Jeff Cline. The young man's enthusiasm and optimistic outlook on life was a refreshing contrast to her own constant questioning of motives. Jeff believed that as long as a person worked hard enough anything was possible. He hadn't learned that caution, suspicion, resignation even, were part of surviving. Jeff raced through life like a yearling colt. He didn't know about barbed-wire fences.

Despite the heat coming on the heels of a day that had begun at six, Chela soon lost herself to the game. The continuous action combined with the rapid changes in possession of the ball by the two teams gave Chela little time to think of anything else. She was vaguely aware of the boys' families sitting along the sidelines, but because she had to be where both Jeff and the team members could communicate with her, she had no time to see how many of the parents had come. She was aware that most of the Mexican boys wore faded tennis shoes, while their opposition had soccer shoes, shin guards inside their socks, new uniforms. That didn't matter. It was skill and enthusiasm and good coaching, not fancy equipment, that won games.

"Have you noticed how surprised our guys are to see girls on the other teams?" Jeff asked as the action slowed following a field goal. "The cultural differences really show up, don't they?"

Chela nodded, not taking her eyes off the boys.

"The old ways are changing, but it takes time. The problem is getting the Mexican girls' parents to allow them to play."

Even as she concentrated on the action, some instinct born from being responsible for her upbringing at an early age went on the alert, warning Chela that she was being watched. She pushed the feeling aside for several minutes, telling herself that as the only female coach on the field, it was likely she would be the object of some interest.

But the feeling persisted. Whoever was watching her wasn't simply doing it out of idle curiosity. The prickling feeling at the nape of her neck built in intensity, warning Chela that somewhere there were eyes that never left her. She felt exposed, vulnerable even. It wasn't until the first half of the game was over that she took time to sweep her eyes slowly, warily, over the knots of people seated on the grass around the playing field.

Suddenly Chela's breath caught, flaring her nostrils, and stopping her hands in a gesture designed to pull the players around her and Jeff. The eyes that met hers from the opposite side of the field were the same ones that had been on her earlier today. The man from the orchard—what was he doing here?

"What's wrong?" Jeff was standing close to her. "You look like you just saw someone from the IRS."

"I don't know who he is," Chela said under cover of the sounds coming from the boys surrounding them. "Do you see the muscular man standing alone? The one in the dark slacks? This is the second time today I've seen him. I think maybe he followed me here."

"Maybe he likes you," Jeff offered. "Come on, Chela. You're a good-looking woman. If I were a little older—I don't know why you think all men are going to bite."

"I don't think all men are going to bite. Just most of them." Chela laughed despite herself and turned her back on the man. "I trust you, don't I?"

"That's just because you've always wanted to be someone's big sister, and I'm sweet and adorable and cuddly. You want me to go over there and ask him if his intentions are honorable? He doesn't look like a dirty old man to me."

"I want you to tell Pablo to stop using his feet to trip the other team." Chela deliberately turned the conversation back to what was necessary. "In a few minutes he'll get tired of staring and leave."

Chela was wrong. Joe Magadan continued his unwavering observation of her throughout the second half of the game. No matter how many times she glanced in his direction, the man was staring at her. It both unnerved Chela and filled her with anger. Didn't he have anything better to do than trail after a woman? If this was his idea of how a man got a woman, this woman, interested in him, he was badly mistaken. Even though half of the blood that flowed through her was that of an Anglo, Chela had enough reason to distrust Anglos.

He wanted something of her. That much instinct told her. Well, when and if he came out with it, Chela already knew what her answer would be.

She wanted nothing to do with the man. Ever.

The soccer game ended with a lopsided victory for

the Mexican boys, much to Jeff's delight and the embarrassment of the superiorly equipped opposition. "I'm going to treat this bunch of future superstars to a soft drink," Jeff proclaimed as he embraced Chela in an enthusiastic bear hug.

"You can't afford it," Chela warned as she disengaged herself, rubbing her arm where it had been smashed against Jeff. "Aren't you the one who told me you couldn't afford a girl friend this summer?"

Jeff's face fell momentarily. "So I won't eat tomorrow. These kids deserve something."

Chela had reached into her back pocket and was pulling out a few bills when she sensed the unexpected presence behind her. She turned quickly to look up into deep nut-brown eyes. Joe Magadan's hand quickly captured her wrist. "This one's on me," he said from the depth of his chest. "Those kids really went after that victory."

Jeff was obviously thrown off by the man's interruption of what had been a private conversation, but Chela reacted in quick anger. She jerked her hand away from its gentle prison and stared back at him, determined not to let her eyes fall before his. "I don't know what you're doing here," she said levelly, her voice giving only a brief glimpse of the anger she felt. "This is between the coach and me. You were watching me earlier today. I don't like it, and I don't appreciate having you show up here."

"I have my reasons," Joe Magadan continued in his deep rumble. Even as he redoubled his own determination not to back down from this tanned woman, he found himself being sucked into eyes much darker, much more intense than he'd expected. Her eyes told him that this was a woman who trusted few people and allowed no one to gain the upper hand. Those remarkable eyes also said something about the woman encased in the slim, athletic body. Somewhere, maybe even deeper than she knew, was something soft and lonely.

"I'm not interested in your reasons," Chela answered slowly. Despite what she was saying, she was interested. In her twenty-seven years she'd met many people, from social workers to public health nurses, from police to politicians even, but this man didn't wear the kind of label that allowed her to identify who or what he was. She could sense his confidence but very little else.

"I think you will be," Joe Magadan countered. "What I need is a little of your time. Give me that."

Chela shook her head. Curiosity wasn't enough of a reason to let go of caution. "The only thing I'm interested in is getting these boys something to drink and making sure they get home before dark."

Joe Magadan waved a fat wallet under her nose. "This will take care of the drinks." Before she could object, he turned toward the assembled team and in fluent Spanish asked where the nearest soft-drink stand was. The excited response from the boys told Chela that it would be almost impossible for her to turn the man down now. Eyes flashing, she pointed to a shopping center across the four-lane thoroughfare and then smiled as the tide of boys swept the arrogant stranger along with them.

"I take it that's the guy who was watching you. Don't ask me to beat him up. He looks like he has a fast one, two, three punch," Jeff said when they were alone. "One thing I can say for him, he has guts."

"Because he's treating a bunch of boys to soft drinks? If he thinks he can win them over that way—"

"I'm not talking about the kids," Jeff interrupted. "It's you he's trying to reach. I saw the way you were looking at him. If looks can kill, I just hope he has his life insurance paid up. You really don't like him, do you?"

"I don't understand him. I don't trust someone who muscles his way in like that without saying anything about himself."

"I think you should listen to what he has to say," Jeff said as he started to fill a mesh bag with soccer balls. "The man isn't going to give up easily. Who knows? Maybe he's an eccentric millionaire who wants to leave his fortune to the first woman he finds with long black hair."

Chela didn't bother to respond to Jeff's outlandish suggestion. She didn't tell the college student that trusting people didn't come easy to her and the last thing she wanted to do was spend any more time with the man who hadn't even told her his name. "Doesn't he have anything better to do with himself?" she asked, the question directed more at herself than at Jeff.

"Ask him," Jeff pressed. "You aren't afraid of him, are you?"

"No. I just don't understand what he's up to."

"You know what I think?" Jeff straightened and turned to face Chela. "I think your curiosity is going to get the best of you. After all, how many strange men have waltzed up to you in your life? If some strange, good-looking woman started talking to me, I'd sure as heck stick around to see what she had in mind."

That's because you don't have any reason to distrust people, Chela thought. *You aren't looking at life through wiser eyes.* "Do all the boys have a way home?" she asked. "I can take some of them."

"I don't know. I guess we'll have to wait until moneybags gets back with them. You know, his Spanish puts mine to shame. Where do you think he learned to speak the language?"

"I have no idea," Chela said shortly before trotting out onto the field to pick up the bright orange cones that served to mark the boundaries of the soccer field. She would have liked to add that learning the answer to that question didn't interest her, but that wasn't true. Most of the Anglos who came in much contact with the migrant workers had learned enough Spanish to get by, but the words flowed easily from the man's mouth. And it wasn't Spanish that came from textbooks. He knew Spanish slang, current jargon that the boys responded to favorably. That came from being around Mexicans.

The trunk of Jeff's little car was filled with equipment by the time the first boys came running back from the shopping center. From their excited speech Chela learned that the stranger had not only bought soft drinks for the entire team but had also picked up the tab for ice-cream cones. Obviously the boys thought him the next best thing to Santa Claus. Chela chose to ignore the man's generosity; instead she questioned the boys until she was sure that all of them either had parents waiting or could get home on their bikes. She held dripping cones for a couple of boys while they ran to get their bikes, and then waved as they started toward the south end of town where a cluster of migrant housing had been built at the far end of one of the orchards.

"You sure you're going to be okay?" Jeff said as he was getting into his car. He nodded in the direction of the shopping center where the stranger was waiting his turn to cross the intersection. "You want me to hang around?"

Chela shook her head and pushed her hair out of her eyes. "I'm not afraid of him," she answered softly.

Jeff was out of sight by the time the man reached her. "You think I bribed the boys, don't you?" he asked abruptly. "And you'd like to know what the hell I'm up to."

"Yes." Chela placed her hands on her hips, fingers spread. "Those boys aren't anything to you. Why did you do that?"

"It doesn't matter. There's just one thing I want you to think about. Kids have pretty good instincts, and they trust me. Look, can we go sit down somewhere? You were on your feet all through the game, and we both logged time in that hot orchard." He pointed toward a wooden picnic table under an oak tree.

For a moment Chela played with the impulse to turn her back on the man and walk out of his life. But something told her that he'd just show up again. Shrugging, she tossed back her head to get her hair off her cheeks and led the way to the table. She straddled one of the benches and sat down the way a cowboy would sit a horse. When she turned to face the man sitting across the table from her, the setting sun caught her hair and revealed red highlights that softened what would have been an unbroken black line. "What do you want?"

"Not so fast. You don't play around, do you? You want to get to the crux of things. Kenneth Duff said that about you."

"Kenneth?" Another woman might have stared in surprise. Instead Chela's gaze became even more intense. She noticed the small scar at the corner of the man's mouth, the slightly askew nose that gave individuality and character to a face that must have stolen many hearts when he was younger and the lines of determination hadn't settled in. "You're talking about the county sheriff."

"That's how I learned about you." The man leaned forward on the table, resting his elbows on the dry, splintered surface. "I know your name is Chela Reola, that you're a teacher with the migrant education system. I also know that if anyone in this valley knows what's going on with the migrants, it's you. They trust you."

Chela locked her eyes with the man's. What was going on inside his head? "I don't know your name."

The man didn't bother to thrust out his hand. "Joe Magadan. Everyone calls me Magadan. Someday maybe you'll want to shake my hand, but I don't think so now."

"You're right." Chela didn't say more. Let the man come to her, reveal himself.

Magadan grunted. "What are you doing here, Magadan? What do you want with me? That's what you're thinking, isn't it?"

Chela didn't have to nod. She knew that her intense, unwavering gaze was telling him more than words could.

"Okay, okay. Damn, this isn't going to be easy. I have to be careful what I say so it comes out right. Look, I think we need to get to know each other better first. I don't want to tip my hand before I know where you stand. What were you going to do after the game?"

"Why?" For the moment at least, Chela felt as if she had the upper hand with Joe Magadan. How long that would last she wasn't going to try to guess.

"Because I want us to spend more time getting used to each other. I was expecting some sweet little schoolteacher. You aren't that at all."

"What am I?" A few minutes ago it would have cost her nothing to walk away from Joe Magadan. She no longer felt that way. The man was a river that ran deep and swift. There might be danger in getting too close to the river, but it was a risk Chela was willing to take.

Magadan was standing up. Chela's side of the table shifted from the loss of his weight. "I have no idea what you are, but I have to find out. I'd like to take you out to dinner."

Chela stood up, too. Somehow, although she would never let him know, she felt better meeting him eye to eye. "And if I say no?"

"Then I'll be everywhere you are tomorrow until you start talking to me. Don't you think it'd be easier this way?"

Chela didn't try to stop her mouth from twitching. She might not trust him, but at least she respected his candor. "I'd like a hamburger."

Chapter Two

Chela was breathing deeply through her nostrils as she waited beside Magadan in the fast-food restaurant. The orange-and-black walls, plastic plants, painted cartoon characters designed to delight youngsters, were closing in on her, not letting her forget that she felt most at home outside. She hadn't been inside a fast-food restaurant in more than a year, but the disgust and wariness she'd felt the last time hadn't left her.

She couldn't blame Magadan for bringing her here. It was close to nine; a quick meal at a place that allowed casual dress was what they needed. Chela was still wearing her soccer-uniform top and faded jeans. Magadan was more conventionally dressed in dark slacks and a knit pullover shirt. She wondered if he was regretting his invitation to take her out or if he was embarrassed.

"You don't like it in here, do you?" Magadan asked after he'd placed their order.

"I didn't know it showed." She had to stand close to him so he could hear her in the crowded space. He wasn't a mountain of a man, but he possessed a substance she couldn't ignore.

"It shows. I can feel your tension. Do you want to eat outside?"

"Yes, please," Chela said, quickly regretting the candor that gave her away. "This is different from where I am most of the time. I've never been able to get used to it."

"I understand. They call it a plastic society. If that's true, then this must be the center of that society. It isn't for you, is it?"

Chela didn't answer him. She barely knew Joe Magadan—how did he know that about her?

Magadan didn't seem to be aware of her discomfort. Instead he was concentrating on making sure the teenage waitress had gotten their order straight. When he'd paid for it and was holding the plastic tray covered with Styrofoam containers in his large hands, he turned and led the way back outside to a group of tables. Nearby was a small play area where several little children were sliding or swinging. "The air's better out here," he said as he was separating a hamburger with pickles from one without. "There aren't many big trucks going by this time of night, so hopefully we won't get the diesel smell."

Chela bit into her hamburger. "Thank you," she said around the squeals of a little girl whose older brother was trying to push her down a slide. "You didn't have to do this."

"Yes I did. Chela, I'm going to lay my cards on the table. At least some of them. I need something from you. I can't tell you everything because if I did, I'm afraid you'd tell me to take a flying leap. Hopefully we can get to know each other well enough that you'll trust my motives."

Chela thought and then decided on honesty. "I don't trust many Anglos."

"You're part Anglo. Your supervisor told me that."

"What are you doing! You talked to my supervisor?" Chela's hand clamped down on her burger, making an indentation in the soft bun.

"It isn't what you think. Relax." Magadan reached for her white knuckles, but Chela shied away.

"How do you know what I'm thinking?" She glared at him. This was his game, but there was nothing in the rules that said she had to respond in a civilized manner around him. "You know I'm half Anglo, but you don't know anything about me. That doesn't add up."

"You're right," Magadan sighed and went back to his dinner. He continued after he'd swallowed. "I knew this was going to be the hard part, getting you to listen to what I have to say, but I have to try. Too much is at stake."

Chela willed her muscles to relax. "You talked to my supervisor," she continued. "Why?"

"You don't go into anything new without doing all the research you can, do you? I'm the same way." He ran a hand through his hair but didn't bother to smooth the locks back into place. The disturbed strands, instead of distracting from his image, gave Chela a more favorable impression of him. The man was thinking about what he was saying, not how he looked. He continued, "Don't worry. Your supervisor didn't tell me much. He said that you'd been working for the system for a little over four years. You take your job home with you. You work for migrant rights and you fight like a tiger to make sure the kids get a decent education. The migrants trust you. That's what I wanted to hear about you."

A piece of the puzzle fell into place. "Why is that important?"

"I'll get to that in a few minutes. Would you tell me why you don't like talking about your father?"

"That, Magadan, is none of your business. It will never be." Ebony eyes left no doubt as to the intensity behind Chela's words. "What else did my supervisor say?"

"Nothing. I mean it. In fact he probably wouldn't have said anything at all except I pretended I already knew you and was curious about why you were working on your own time during the summer. You were teaching English to those men out in the orchard today. That's not in your contract. I asked your supervisor about that. That's when he told me you were dedicated, intense, trusted by the migrants. That's the same thing the sheriff told me."

"Is that a compliment?" Since they'd sat down, Magadan hadn't dropped his eyes once. The fact that he was willing to meet her intense scrutiny was a point in his favor.

Magadan laughed. "I guess it depends on whose side of the fence you're on. Most orchardists want workers who are content with their lives, not workers who are learning that there's more to reach for once they have an education."

"That's the owners' problem," Chela snapped. "I don't think it's right to bring workers here from Mexico, work them seven days a week, pay minimum wage, and then call the immigration authorities before payday. An orchardist should treat his employees the way every other employer treats his employees."

"Wait a minute." Magadan's eyes seemed to narrow. "Not all orchardists take advantage of their workers. Some are decent."

"Not enough," Chela challenged. "Orchardists hire the coyotes in the first place. Don't tell me it doesn't go on. I know it does."

Magadan leaned forward, his face less than a foot away in the night. "I know it happens," he said softly. "You probably know more about it than anyone except the migrants themselves. That's why I'm here."

For over a minute Chela said nothing. Despite the blinking neon light behind them, Magadan's features had become blurred, but there was no mistaking the intensity in his eyes. Maybe now, finally, they were getting to the heart of why Magadan was here. "Do you work for immigration?" she asked.

"What would you do if I said yes?"

"Walk away."

"Why?"

Chela sighed. It was late and she was tired. Being with Magadan with his determined lines and bold eyes had her on the alert. He had asked a question that couldn't be answered quickly or easily. "I believe that the system the way it works now has flaws. Agriculture in this country relies on migrant labor, but not all of the workers are here legally. Since they can't wade through the red tape, the immigration authorities deport the illegals they find. It makes criminals out of people who are only trying to earn a living. Something has to change."

"You believe in that strongly, don't you?"

This time Chela's sigh was a little less civilized. "My grandparents were migrants. I was born in a migrant camp. The work killed my mother."

"Oh." Magadan had started to take another bite of his burger, but he seemed unaware that it was still a few inches from his mouth. "I didn't know."

"Do you work for immigration?"

Magadan shook his head, and although Chela could barely make out his features, she believed him. He still wasn't telling her everything, but at least ground was being broken. "Whom do you work for?"

"Chela, I can't tell you that. I told you I can't tell you everything about what I'm doing. That's one of the main things."

"I think that's the main thing," she said, body still, senses alert. What Magadan was saying or not saying intrigued her. He had sought her out for a purpose. But he wasn't willing to reveal himself. Did she dare get any closer to the man?

"Maybe. Let me ask you something else. Do you know any coyotes?"

"You work for the police. That's it, isn't it? That's how you know Kenneth Duff." Chela frowned at her own words. "But why do the police care about coyotes? They never did before."

"What they do is illegal. Chela, you know migrants. You must know how many of them have been cheated by coyotes."

Chela knew. She could point at any illegal in the orchard and guess he was here because of the effort of someone who, for a fee, would smuggle workers across the border to the agricultural work centers. Unfortunately, once coyotes had their money, most of them couldn't care less what happened to the illegals. Promised jobs might never materialize. Coyotes sometimes disappeared before delivering their "clients," leaving both workers and farm owners in need of laborers to suffer the consequences. Neither the illegal nor the orchardist would dare press charges.

"Is this what our discussion is about?" Chela asked. "You're after coyotes?"

"Let me ask you one more question before I answer that," Magadan pressed. "What would your response be if I said I was?"

Chela admitted it was a good question. No matter what her opinion of them, if a coyote made good on his promises, the migrant stood a chance of improving his standard of living. "I don't know," she answered honestly. "Some migrants need them."

"They don't need Ray Kohl."

Chela stopped breathing. She dropped what was left of her hamburger, placed her hands on the table, and pushed herself to her feet. She turned her back on Magadan and walked on silent feet through the low fencing leading to the miniature playground. She didn't take a breath until she'd wrapped her hands around the chain holding the leather swing seat in place. She tossed her hair back and stared skyward, making out the first glimmer of stars in the distance.

Kohl had survived her father's ruin. He was probably the only one who knew who her father was. But he was more, much more than that. Behind her she could sense Magadan's presence but didn't turn to acknowledge him. Ray Kohl. She didn't know that his name was ever spoken outside the migrant camps and orchards. The name gave both children and men nightmares, and yet no one had found a way of escaping the nightmare.

"You know him, don't you?" Magadan whispered behind her.

A barely perceptible nod disturbed the sleek line of hair trailing down Chela's back. "What is he to you?" she asked.

"A monster. He has to be stopped."

Chela whirled back around. "What do you care? He can't touch you."

"I'm a human being, damn it!" Magadan's hands grabbed both naked arm and long strands of hair. "I know he has to be stopped. But I need your help."

"Me?" Chela was shaking, not because she was afraid of the man gripping her but because the intensity of emotion she felt had to find some expression. What she felt for Kohl went beyond hatred, beyond loathing. "I can't stop Kohl. There's money behind him."

"I know. The money of some orchardists who need workers and don't care how they get here or how much the migrants are cheated by Kohl. But there are other orchard owners who won't stoop to that. They want him out of business."

"I wish I could believe that," Chela said softly, firmly. She wasn't going to think about her link to Kohl. "But I don't trust any of the owners." Chela tried to break free, but Magadan was gripping her arms with a strength she couldn't fight; yet it didn't frighten her. Over the years, as Chela aligned herself more and

more with her mother's people, she'd cut herself off
from contact with men outside the barrios and orchards. Being touched by one of those men evoked a
reaction she didn't understand. His face, his mouth,
were only a few inches away. She needed time to ana-
lyze her reaction to his nearness, to question why his
touch neither frightened nor repulsed her. But this
wasn't the time. Magadan wanted something of her
that had to do with a name she associated with everything evil. That was what demanded her attention.

"Listen to me," Magadan was saying. "That's why I
talked to your supervisor and other people like the
sheriff. I know Kohl, but I don't know how he operates. I don't think anyone really does, even those he
works for. But you—you're part of the migrant community—"

"Is that a compliment?"

"That isn't the point. It's enough that I know where
your loyalties lie. Chela, you said there's money behind
him. I want you to understand that there is also money
behind a drive to put him out of business. He's ruthless
and cruel. He has no humanity." Magadan shook his
head. "I've given up trying to understand what makes
the man tick. All I know is that he has to be put out of
business. I can't get close to him, but you can."

Chela pulled out of Magadan's grip, knowing that it
wouldn't have been possible if he hadn't allowed it.
She took a deep breath, gaining control over her emotions. "I'm not close to Kohl. You can't believe that."

"Maybe I said that wrong," Magadan acknowledged.
"I don't for a minute believe you'd sit down at the
same table with that animal. But you know the people

he deals with, the ones he's cheated. Come on Chela, don't deny it. You're aware of every illegal in this valley, where they're staying, how they got here."

Chela wasn't going to deny that. Neither was she going to let Magadan take advantage of her knowledge. He wasn't willing to tell her enough about his motives, so why should she trust him?

As if he'd read her thoughts, he shrugged. "We're going pretty fast, aren't we?" he admitted. "I've known you less than a day, and already I'm pushing you hard. Look, why don't I take you home and let you sleep on it? You know I want Kohl out of business. You know I'm part of a group with the money to charge him with breaking the law and making that charge stick. What we need are some facts; get him to show his hand. That's where I want you to come in."

"You're asking too much. I don't even know you."

"Give me time." Magadan took a half step toward her and then stopped. "Don't turn your back on what I'm saying, Chela. Give yourself time to get to know me."

"Maybe you work with Kohl."

Magadan laughed harshly. "Maybe I do. I didn't think about that, but it could look as if I'm trying to find out if anyone is going to blow the whistle on the operation. Look, I said it before, but those kids on your soccer team trusted me enough to let me buy them drinks. Can't you bank on their instincts?"

"Maybe." Chela's teeth were exposed momentarily as she gave Magadan a rueful grin. "You said you'd talked to people about me. Now maybe I should do the same thing about you."

Once again Chela sensed the man becoming tense, but his words hid what his body language was telling her. "I can't argue your right to do that. And I can't stop you. But I don't think you're going to find out much. I have reasons for keeping a low profile. Look, do you want to finish your dinner?"

Chela shook her head. Thoughts of Ray Kohl had chased food from her mind. "I'm tired. I'm not going to make any decisions now," she pointed out. "My Jeep's back at the park. Will you take me there, or shall I walk?"

"I'd rather take you to your place," Magadan said as they were getting into his pickup. "I haven't had time to see where you live."

"But you will." If the man was that interested in her, she had no doubt that he wasn't done learning all he could about her. "I don't spend much time there," she continued, aware that Magadan had glanced at the distance separating them in the vehicle. "It's where I keep my belongings, where I go to sleep. But there's always something to take me out of it."

"Like finding a job at a day-care center for a woman who doesn't speak English. That's something else I've learned about you."

Chela said nothing. She'd already been more candid with Magadan than any other man she'd met. It was time to retreat into silence. She stared out at the darkened streets, thinking about the distance separating her from this mysterious man. Chela hadn't been born with a hands-off approach when it came to men, but she wasn't part of the mainstream of life. A shopping center was as foreign to her as a Jeep was to most women. She simply didn't come in contact with men near her own age, men who might someday take away the feeling that she would walk through life alone. There were men who showed interest in her, of course, but Chela had no time for casual affairs, for men who wanted nothing more than an attractive woman to hold in the night and discard once the conquest had been made.

She knew she was existing in some kind of limbo, wanting more and yet not knowing what that something was. She felt the boundaries of her life, wanted to reach beyond, but didn't know how to take the necessary steps. She didn't blame her mother for what she'd become because Chela's mother never had the energy or education or opportunity to fight her way out of the orchards. She couldn't blame her father for what she was because it was hard to blame a man she barely knew. Wanting nothing to do with her father came later when she learned the kind of man he was. Maybe, Chela sometimes thought, the fault lay with the older couple who had taken her in after her mother died.

William and Carolyn Roberts made sure the shy, frightened girl learned to speak English and went to public school. And when her quick mind hungered for knowledge, her teachers fed that hunger until Chela was one of the best students in her class. Her foster parents worked with counselors to ensure that Chela received several college scholarships. They provided her with food, clothing, and a warm bed. And when they lacked the ability to replace a mother's love, Chela learned to accept that.

William and Carolyn both died within a year of each

other just after Chela started college, and the lonely girl was shuffled off by well-meaning authorities to the college dorm where she had few friends and buried herself in the task of becoming a teacher. But not just an ordinary teacher. Chela found a job as an aide to the college Spanish teacher and honed her skills. By the time she graduated, she knew she wanted to be involved in migrant education. An education had given her the freedom to leave the orchards; she wanted to give others that same choice.

And yet it was a lonely life. Dealing with basic concerns such as teaching a new language to people who needed help understanding the different culture they found themselves in was a responsibility she took seriously. She tried to tell herself that she was doing enough, experiencing enough, that it should satisfy her. But it hadn't, and a man named Joe Magadan was forcing her to face her restlessness.

Magadan felt something for people whose roots were different from his. That he couldn't keep from Chela. She couldn't deny the caring, the commitment she sensed about the man. She trusted her instincts in that regard. She believed that if she asked him, he would say he thought of her as a woman first and the color of her skin second.

But what kind of a woman? Was Magadan's interest in her only because she provided the link he needed with migrants in order to expose Kohl?

Chela had never asked herself that question about a man before. She had no idea how to go about finding the answer.

"I want to see you next week," Magadan said when

he'd parked his truck next to her Jeep. "That'll give you time to find out some things about me. Don't close your mind to this, Chela. We might not be able to change the world, but we can put one animal out of operation."

Chela opened the door, but instead of sliding out, she turned to find Magadan's eyes in the night. "I'm not promising anything."

"I understand. There's one other thing I want you to know: I won't ask you to do anything that's dangerous."

"Dangerous?" Chela laughed. "If you believe that, then you don't know Kohl."

Chela saw his right hand reach toward her but didn't shy from the contact. His fingers gave warmth to her arm. "I wouldn't let anything happen to you," he whispered.

Her arm remained warm long after Chela climbed into her Jeep and drove off. Neither of them had said anything about how or when Magadan would be getting in touch, but by now Chela knew he would show up when he felt the time was right.

Chela pulled into her driveway and parked her Jeep in the carport connected to the small house she was buying on a quiet country road skirting the orchards. There were no neighbors in sight, only a wheat field on one side and vacant land in the hands of an out-of-state holding company on the other. Someday, Chela suspected, the vacant land would be bought by a developer, and she'd move on to a more rural setting.

The house itself was more than forty years old, thrown together by a man with confidence in his ability but not much money. She'd painted both inside and out and polished the hardwood floors until they glistened. Because she had no neighbors, Chela had never bothered with curtains. She loved to watch the sun stream in through the open expanse, catch dust particles in the air, and bounce off the white walls. It had been the wood stove in the living room that allowed Chela to see beyond the neglected walls and a leaking roof. Even in summer she gravitated toward it, keeping her favorite rocking chair and table piled with books next to the stove's cozy presence.

She wasn't surprised that Magadan hadn't seen her house. Because she cherished her privacy, she rented a post-office box and used that when receiving correspondence from the education system. Except for a couple of student teachers who were now employed elsewhere, no one from work had been to her house.

Although Chela had taken pains in finding furnishings and wall decorations that reflected her love of the out-of-doors and earth colors, she seldom took time to study the paintings of several local artists she'd bought or the rough-finished redwood coffee table she found after months of searching. But as she kicked off her tennis shoes and slid her feet along the smooth wood floor, she found herself wondering what Magadan's reaction would be to her home. His stylish slacks and nearly new shirt, as well as the immaculate condition of his powerful pickup, revealed him as someone who could afford whatever he wanted.

Chela walked into the small bathroom with its old fashioned bathtub set up on sturdy legs. She started running water in the tub, eager to remove pollen and weed seeds from her flesh. There were grass stains on her denims, but she'd long ago learned not to become unduly concerned about that.

As she started shampooing her hair, she couldn't help but wonder what Magadan's reaction had been to a woman who carried residues of an orchard around with her. He was probably much more accustomed to women who didn't have to rake their hands through their hair periodically to make sure they hadn't picked up a twig from a pear tree or need to check under their nails for dirt, Chela admitted as she slid her fingertips along her hair. There was no denying it. Her hands were utilitarian, not glamorous.

The man had remarkable hands, large for his size; yet there was nothing clumsy about them. Chela remembered how Magadan's fingers felt on her upper arm, the warmth that radiated from him and into her. Was that why she hadn't turned her back on him when he approached her with too many questions and not enough answers? Was there a magnetism to him that kept people from saying no to him?

Maybe that was why her thoughts wouldn't leave Magadan and his large hands, his bold eyes, and the warmth that radiated from him. Because so much of him was still a mystery, she couldn't put a label on the man. She knew he wasn't an immigration officer. Something told her he wasn't a policeman, although that was yet another question he hadn't answered. He was a man with money, a man who had no love for a certain coyote and was willing to spend money to rid the area of that man. Other than that Chela knew nothing.

She didn't even know if he had a wife.

Magadan pushed the lever in his truck that activated the automatic garage-door opener and pulled into the spacious garage. After lowering the door behind him, he unlocked the door leading from the garage to the house and stepped into a tiled entryway. He picked up his mail from where it had fallen through the slot and then lowered his solid frame onto a leather couch. He propped his feet up on a glass-topped coffee table, oblivious of his housekeeper's efforts to keep the house spotless, despite its owner's casual disdain for expensive furnishings.

Magadan had been back in the valley and living in the home vacated by his predecessor for several months, but other than making sure his mail would be delivered here, he'd done little to turn the house into a home he felt comfortable in. That, he decided when he thought about it at all, would come later. For the present he was fully occupied with the task of undoing the damage caused by his predecessor. The transactions that put him into a deserted but completely furnished home were known only by a handful of people, and they were either lawyers or bankers who knew the wisdom of keeping their own counsel. Even the middle-aged woman who came in once a week to undo the damage of a bachelor knew almost nothing about her employer.

For a few minutes Magadan thought he was going to be able to concentrate on mail that dealt with stock reports, a report from his accountant, and a few bills, but as he discarded an advertisement from the local

Grange, he had to admit that ebony eyes and not financial matters were what was on his mind.

She won't be what you expect, the sheriff had said. Damn the old goat! If that wasn't an understatement, Magadan didn't know what was. Not a word about her being one of the most arresting creatures he'd ever seen. Untamed, the sheriff called her. But that didn't say it all either. The plain truth of the matter was, Chela Reola didn't fit any cubbyhole Magadan had ever been aware of. He'd met enough women in his thirty-four years to think he knew just about all there was to know about them. There were clinging vines, independent career women, insecure child-women, and bitter creatures who looked at all men with suspicion.

Magadan couldn't for the life of him figure out what Chela thought of men. There was a certain wariness to her that told him she'd had some bad experiences in her life, but that didn't mean the warmth and giving had been sucked out of her. Somehow, he felt, there was a sensitive core hidden behind the dark eyes, but that core was kept well under control by a woman who'd learned that she had to be strong and independent in order to survive in the world she'd forged for herself.

Somewhere along the line she'd stopped accepting people at face value. If he was ever going to get her to trust him, he was going to have to prove himself. But that was going to be difficult when the very nature of their relationship prevented total honesty.

Magadan kicked off his shoes without bothering to untie them and wandered into the den-turned-office that served as the focal point for his activities these days. He dialed the number of Phillip McAndrews without having to look it up.

"I can't tell you if it's going to work," Magadan said after he and the fifty-year-old community kingpin had exchanged pleasantries. "I've made the contact, but I don't know if she's going to buy our story."

"She? You're dealing with a woman? Are you sure that's necessary?"

"I'm sure," Magadan answered. "I've done enough poking around to know that a woman named Chela Reola is our best bet—"

"Chela?" Phillip interrupted. "She'll trust you about as far as she can throw you. You'll never get her to go along with anything. She keeps to herself."

"I had dinner with her tonight. Give me time. Look, I spent an hour with the sheriff the other day. He agreed with us that the Mexicans around here aren't going to give us anything that would expose Kohl. They're too intimidated by him. And you better believe certain orchardists we can both name are going to protect that snake. He'll blow the whistle on them if the law comes after him, and they know it. He isn't going to go down alone unless we do this right."

"Are you sure you have the sheriff's cooperation? We have a lot at stake here, you know," Phillip said nervously. "If he doesn't press charges—"

"Kenneth is with us all the way. And so is the DA. I'm a little concerned because the DA is going to want names blasted all over the newspapers when this business comes to court. It'll be a feather in his cap for him if he pulls it off. He'll want everyone to think he was responsible for getting us involved."

"You keep my name out of the paper," Phillip warned. "You're new here. You don't have as much at stake as I do. The orchardists are a powerful group."

"I have enough at stake," Magadan pointed out wearily. He wasn't crazy about working with the publicity-shy McAndrews, but the older man had connections and local political clout Magadan didn't. "Besides, if this works out the way we want it to, we aren't going to be the ones sticking our necks out. Chela Reola is."

"Does she know that? I think we need to clarify that with her. Arrange a meeting with the three of us. I respect her too much to be anything less than honest. Does she know what Kohl is capable of?"

"She knows, all right. I don't think she's afraid, but neither does she trust me. Not that I can blame her given the little information I've told her. Look, it's late. I just wanted to keep you abreast of what's going on. Right now I'm giving her time to think things over. I have to do that."

"No way. Don't ever give a woman time, especially that one," Phillip warned. "That's one savvy lady. I'll tell you what I'd do if I were in your place. Turn on the charm. Get her eating out of your hand, and you're home free. A woman in love will do anything for her man."

"It's a good thing I have no intention of taking your advice," Magadan said before putting an end to the conversation. "I've never heard of that trick working on a woman. I know it isn't going to work with Chela."

What would work on Chela Reola? Magadan wondered later as he got ready for bed. He could imagine her expression if he sent her flowers or invited her out to a fancy restaurant. Instead of melting from the effect of his charms, she would be instantly suspicious. *Sorry, Phillip,* Magadan thought. *Even if I have charm, which I'm not sure I have, it isn't going to convince this particular woman that I'm on the up-and-up.*

Flowers and a romantic evening—had Chela ever had that experience? Magadan thought of her strong hands with their short clipped nails and doubted that she'd ever been inside the valley's exclusive restaurants. Then he thought of questioning ebony eyes with something vulnerable and hungry flickering deep inside them and acknowledged a desire to give her that evening. Then he chided himself. This wasn't the way he should be thinking. This was a business arrangement, nothing more.

Chapter Three

Magadan had given Chela a week to learn what she could about him, but it could have been a year for all the good the week did her. Jackson County wasn't what could be called an urban center, but with a city of some 30,000 as the county's hub, plus a half dozen small towns surrounding Medford, it was impossible for Chela to learn anything about a man who didn't even have his number listed in the telephone book. It bothered her to realize that Magadan had been aware of how hard he would be to trace, but in a way she understood. Some people required a low profile in their lifestyle. Magadan was one of them.

When Chela deliberately mentioned that she'd been approached by a self-confident yet secretive man, her supervisor apologized for having told Magadan what he did about her. Unfortunately the older man was unable to answer any questions. "He came into my office wearing a suit that isn't going to be found in a catolog. He was so self-assured that maybe I let it intimidate me. He said something about being involved in law enforcement. He expected me to answer his questions, and I fell right into his hands. I admit I was eager to cooperate with whatever agency he represented. What did he want anyhow?"

Chela didn't answer. What she and Magadan had discussed was none of the man's business. Besides, she had learned long ago that it was better to keep certain things to oneself. She would continue going into the orchards and barrios and wait for Magadan to get in touch with her.

He walked back into her life much the same way he'd entered it. Chela had been in one of the more isolated orchards, talking to a worker who was terrified of appearing in court about a traffic ticket. She'd assured the man that she would go to court with him and was walking back through the silent rows of trees to the shed where she'd left her Jeep when Magadan appeared, seemingly out of nowhere.

Instead of breaking the silence, he simply waited as she came closer. Today he was dressed in jeans and an unironed but fairly new shirt.

"It's hot," Magadan observed objectively. "Don't you ever wish you worked in an air-conditioned office?"

Chela glanced down at the long expanse of denim-clad leg. "I'd have to wear a dress. I don't own any."

"You don't own a dress?"

Chela allowed herself a smile. "Almost. I have a couple of sun dresses, something with a blazer I bought for when the superintendent of schools comes calling, and slacks during the school year, but I live in these in the summer."

Magadan didn't come closer, but his eyes made a

quick decision. Size 10. And she would look good in any color, particularly intense ones that wouldn't be lost next to her own rich coloring and shining black hair. "Have you had enough time?" he asked.

Despite the sudden shift in conversation, Chela knew what Magadan was talking about. Instantly she pushed aside the image of a strong, competent man standing close to her in an orchard empty except for birds and small rodents. She dug her tennis shoes into the rich bottom soil of the Bear Creek valley and reached out to touch the hard, immature surface of a sun-warmed d'Anjou pear. "You knew I wouldn't learn anything about you," she pointed out. "Your name isn't in the phone book, but I didn't expect it to be."

"I have my reasons for having it unlisted. Forget that. That isn't important." Magadan waved away his own impatience and nodded in the direction of a shed surrounded by farm equipment. He fell in line behind Chela as she walked through a carpet of wild mustard toward it. "It's so quiet here," he said softly. "There's a peace to the orchards. Does it bother you that I don't have my face plastered all over town?"

"The trees are doing their work now. It'll get busy when the pears are ripe," Chela said just as softly. "It bothers me that you expect me to take everything you say at face value. You want me to do something for you, but you won't even tell me who you are, what you do. You played the same game with my supervisor."

Magadan waited until they reached a stack of baled straw just outside the shed. Chela climbed onto one of the bales and sat cross-legged on it. Taking her lead, he chose a bale next to hers, positioning himself so that nothing that might show in her eyes would escape him. Behind her he saw the gnarled branches of endless trees silhouetted against the summer sun. "What do you want me to tell you?" he asked.

"I don't know. I don't even know why I'm talking to you." But maybe she did. The man sitting cross-legged near her was fascinating, not because she knew so little about him, but because she was reacting toward him in a way she barely understood.

"I don't know why you haven't told me to take a flying leap either," Magadan admitted. "Except maybe you believe how I feel about a creature like Kohl. That's one thing I can level with you about. I want the man out of operation. I'm willing to do whatever it takes to accomplish that."

"But you won't tell me why you don't want him around. Why should you care?"

Magadan sighed. "Several reasons. I was near the Rio Grande last year. I wound up doing some interpreting for a family Kohl had taken across the border and deserted. Of course, he had their money before he took off. Two adults and five kids stranded illegally with everything they owned on their backs and Kohl getting fat from what they'd given him to get them into California."

Chela frowned. His words may have been quiet, but she could see the anger and outrage in his clenched jaw, his narrowed eyes. "And that's why you're after Kohl? Because of something he did to a family you didn't know?"

Magadan laughed. "That makes me sound like the white knight, doesn't it? No. That was the first time I'd heard Kohl's name. Since moving here I've learned a lot more about that bastard. The most I can tell you at this time is that I've had dealings with a couple of local orchardists who worked with Kohl. He provided them with illegal workers. In turn both he and the orchardists robbed the illegals blind. Immigration showed up just before payday and hauled them back to Mexico. No human being should treat another that way. Whether they were legal or not, they worked, they deserved to be paid. He has to be stopped."

"He?" Chela spat bitterly. "What about the orchardists? Or are they too powerful to touch?"

"Maybe. Chela, you've lived here most of your life. You know how much influence the orchardists have in this valley. The fruit harvest is an important part of the area's economic base. The legal system isn't going to blow the whistle on them unless they have an airtight case and the money to counter the orchardists' high-priced lawyers. But if Kohl is put out of business, then their supply is cut off. They'll get the message: Either clean up their act or risk being exposed the way Kohl was."

"You said you've had dealings with the orchardists," Chela said warily. "What kind of dealings?"

"I'm afraid I'm not at liberty to tell you that. Look, I haven't given you any reason to believe I'm anything but a law-abiding citizen, have I? Let's just say I'm working in conjunction with the law enforcement system."

Chela met the man's narrowed, wary eyes. She knew that most men dropped their eyes when they were lying, but there was nothing tentative about the way

Magadan returned her stare. Were his eyes telling the truth? Did she dare believe him? A part of her that was soft and deeply buried cried "yes," but the part of Chela that challenged her to fight for migrant rights was wary.

A gust of wind found its way down the rows of trees. Chela waited until the rustling branches had spent themselves before she spoke. "You have something to do with law enforcement? That doesn't tell me much."

Magadan groaned. "There are some other things about me you should know. You got time?"

Chela sat motionless, absorbing both words and impressions as Magadan told about the only son of a successful lawyer who cut his teeth on legal defenses and fact-gathering, much as other boys learned about sports and cars. "My father was a lawyer for twenty years before becoming one of the most outspoken district attornies the state has ever seen. He loved his work; he fought to make sure that victims of crimes weren't forgotten. He didn't have much use for repeat criminals. Maybe my father was the modern-day equivalent of the Lone Ranger. I thought he was about the greatest man I'd ever known. I know I've never admired anyone as much as I admired him. For a long time I thought I was going to be a lawyer, too, but when I got to law school, I discovered I was much more interested in business than law."

"You're a businessman?"

"Something like that. Let's just say I have a certain knack for sniffing out opportunities and turning them to my advantage. I had to start out small, but I now have enough capital to take bigger risks." Magadan frowned. "Forget I said that. I'm not here to toot my own horn."

"I don't know what you're here for. Are you going to arrest Kohl? Do you have that authority?" Chela straightened and then recrossed her legs. She rested her arms on her bent knees and folded her hands together, waiting.

"I'm here because you are. Because there's a fly in the ointment, and you're the one to get rid of him."

Chela's laugh cut sharply through the gentle orchard sounds. "I'm a means to an end, is that it? Someone you can use." A second later she was on her feet, brushing hay off her clothes as she turned her back on Magadan. "I've seen one user in my life. I don't want anything to do with another."

Chela started to walk toward the nearest row of trees, but Magadan stopped her. He grabbed her shoulders, biting down with his fingers to keep the wiry young woman from pulling away. "I'm not a user. I wouldn't take advantage of you."

Chela whirled back around. "How can I believe that? You won't tell me anything about yourself, anything important."

"Because I can't." Magadan's hands dropped to his side. For a moment he seemed at a loss for words. "At this stage of the plan, I just can't. I'd jeopardize too much hard work."

Chela took a backward step, trying to decrease the impact of the agony she heard in the strong, competent man's voice. But once again Magadan reached for Chela. His hands snaked out as if afraid she'd shy away before he could capture her. She'd started to back off, but he was too quick for her. Magadan gripped her wrists, pulling her toward him. When she was less than a foot away, he pulled her hands downward and close to his sides so she was thrown off balance. Chela felt his breath on the side of her face and stiffened. Gentle, caressing touches from men weren't the kind of contact she was used to. Magadan was rough in his handling of her, rough enough to alarm her. And yet, because she retained the memory of the honesty that lived in his eyes, she didn't try to escape. Instead she stood, trembling slightly, waiting for him to make the next move.

Magadan hadn't intended on kissing Chela, but with her soft lips only inches away, he surrendered to the impulse. He pulled down and back with his hands, drawing her ever closer. She thrust her chin out, but the defiant act only made him more determined.

Chela felt his lips on hers and barely suppressed a gasp as she acknowledged her body responding to the contact. She kept her eyes open, body tense, as the gentle whispering touch became more intimate. His face was so close that it was no more than a blur but not so fuzzy that she couldn't see that his eyes, too, were open. Chela stopped resisting the pull on her wrists and took the half step that brought their bodies together. Now she could concentrate on what was happening without being distracted by the almost painful pressure of his fingers on her wrists. She felt his body warmth through her, reaching the unencumbered breasts beneath the thin fabric. Unless she was representing the school district, Chela didn't usually wear a bra. She hated any kind of confinement. Now that decision was working against her natural reserve.

What would it feel like to close her eyes, let her body come in full contact with Magadan's? Even as she was asking how she dared ask such a question, her eyes were slowly closing. There was no breeze blowing in the orchard, allowing the humidity of the hot day to settle around everything it touched. But Chela wasn't aware of the sticky, pungent air. Her thoughts were telescoping down until the core of her consciousness went no further than her mouth, her breasts, female flesh hungering for the touch of male flesh.

Because Magadan's hands were around her wrists and not against her back, Chela didn't feel completely possessed by him. There was a certain sense of freedom, the knowledge that she was a willing participant in what was happening.

Why she should now be willing to let happen something she'd been wary of for years didn't, at this moment, occur to her. What was left to concentrate on was the knowledge that she'd been hungry for this kind of contact, lonely because there'd been no one to share herself with.

Chela had made decisions that set her apart from close contact with a man she could give herself to. Most of the time she was unaware of the loneliness her decision had sentenced her to. Now, however, there was no denying that.

She became aware of a subtle shifting of position but didn't open her eyes. It was much preferable to acknowledge Magadan's hands working their way up her arms, touching her shoulders, and finally coming around behind her back. Tentatively, shyly, Chela lifted her limp arms and allowed them to find a home around Magadan's waist.

She was no longer holding her neck stiffly. Instead she let the pressure from Magadan's lips push her head backward slightly, increasing the sensation of being pliable in the arms of the kind of man she wasn't sure existed.

It wasn't until Magadan's hands found the flesh under her blouse that Chela pulled herself back to the reality of orchard heat and buzzing insects. She pulled firmly away, opened her eyes, and faced him. It took every ounce of strength she possessed not to flee into the safety of the trees.

"That was nice," Magadan whispered. "I didn't know it was going to happen, but I'm not going to apologize."

"It isn't going to happen again." Was that her voice shaking like a young girl on her first date?

"I doubt it, Chela. Is that so wrong?"

Instead of answering, Chela reached out and brought a pear branch close to her face. She stared as if fascinated at the vibrant green growth. "Are you sure Kohl can be stopped?"

"That's what you want to talk about? All right. We'll play the game your way today. But there's something happening between us, Chela. I don't think you can deny that forever."

"Nothing's happening between us!" Chela shot out in fear. "You're Anglo."

Magadan came a step closer. "So are you, Chela," he said gently. "At least half of you is. Why are you afraid to admit it?"

"I'm not afraid." Her hands were clenched tightly around the tree branch as if she could use the tree's life force to still the emotions raging inside her. "I have reasons for hating certain things about me, that's all."

Magadan reached out as if to touch her but stopped just short of contact as if he was aware of the fragile hold she had on herself. "I'd like you to tell me about it," he said in the same gentle tone.

"I don't think so." Chela's eyes met his because she'd learned to face life head on, but there was no way she could hide the agony in the dark orbs. "You aren't the only one with secrets, Magadan."

"I had that coming, didn't I?" he acknowledged. "Look, you asked about Kohl—maybe that's the only safe subject we can find—but I don't want to talk about it here, now. There's someone I want you to meet."

"Who? I haven't promised anything—"

"I know that," Magadan interrupted sharply. "But the man is, shall we say, my partner in this scheme. I think you know him anyway. Phillip McAndrews."

If Chela was already tense, she became more so now. "Phillip McAndrews is an orchardist. How do you know him?"

"Through the Chamber of Commerce. McAndrews might not be your idea of man of the year, but I'm told he's one of the most progressive orchardists in the valley."

"He could do more." Chela ran a weary hand over her eyes. An instinct for survival still told her to back out of whatever Magadan and McAndrews were planning, but Chela wasn't one for running away. If there was a way of putting an end to a coyote who dealt in farm laborers as if they were merchandise and not human beings, she was willing to take certain chances. Besides, something of a kiss lingered, holding her where she was as firmly as any rope. "Does he want to meet me?"

"Yes. He's arranged to meet with both of us tomorrow night at his house."

Phillip McAndrews's house—it was close, too close to another house Chela wanted to avoid for the rest of her life. But personal emotions had no place intruding on this particular meeting. "Would I have to wear a dress?"

"Magadan laughed. "No, I don't think you'll have to wear a dress. Then, you'll come?"

"What time should I be there?"

As quickly as it had started, Magadan's laugh stopped. "I'd like to pick you up."

Chela shook her head firmly. "I don't tell many people where I live," she said. "You have a long way to go before I tell you that, Magadan."

Chapter Four

Magadan deliberately arrived at Phillip McAndrews's place a half hour before Chela was expected. He and the publicity-shy orchardist had exchanged pleasantries and were now sharing a drink in the deeply masculine den of Phillip's sprawling house. Phillip had explained that his wife was at the country club that evening for some benefit show, and they wouldn't be interrupted.

"You know," Phillip was saying, "I kind of feel sorry for my wife. I don't think she had any idea that being married to an orchardist would mean having to put up with a man who smelled like fertilizer and pesticides. She thinks we should stay here or at the country club all the time and the orchards can function without us. She can't stand to have me around when I come in with mud under my fingernails and the truck looking like its been rode hard and put away wet. But pears aren't going to make it to the packing houses without a lot of hard work on someone's part, mainly mine."

"Don't forget luck." Magadan took a sip of his rum and Coke and eased back in the comfortable chair, letting the day's labors ease from his body. He'd dressed in brown slacks and a three-year-old shirt, hoping his casual dress would soften the contrast between the expensive McAndrews home and the jeans he expected Chela to wear. Not that he minded the faded denim stretched across her small bottom. The thought of her soft tank top sliding softly over her breasts made him glance at the clock, eager to see her coming through the door. It wasn't the way he expected to be reacting to his potential partner, but to deny his feelings would be to lie to himself.

Phillip was going on about his current problem of being able to get an adequate supply of pesticides to be applied by a local crop duster. Magadan nodded, only vaguely aware of the brief comments he was making. A hot, serious—to him—romance had ended rather abruptly just as he was leaving Mexico earlier this year. Since moving to the valley, Magadan hadn't dated or shown much interest in women. He was beginning to wonder whether he'd been too single-minded in his business ventures to the detriment of a personal life. At least that's what his ex-girl friend had told him. "You're too intense. You have this thing about changing the world," she'd said that last day. "Someday you're going to have to stop long enough to smell the roses, or life is going to pass you by. Stop trying to prove something. Listen to the beating of your heart."

Well, his heart was beating tonight. In fact he'd been aware of its steady pulse ever since he'd held Chela in his arms in the orchard yesterday. What was it with that woman? Did she possess some special spark, some captivating quality that set her apart from other women, or had he simply been without a woman too long?

"That's about enough shoptalk for one night," Phillip said as he replenished their drinks. "So you really got Chela Reola to come here tonight. That surprised me."

"So you said. How come?"

"You don't know about her father, do you? I'm not surprised. The fact is, I know damn little myself. Just that he's alive and around here, but they apparently don't have anything to do with each other. That certainly isn't the sort of thing she'd be likely to talk about."

"Don't play games with me, Phillip," Magadan said more sharply than he'd intended. "Is there something I should know?"

"You know all I do. He's American, of course. There's been speculation about his identity, but she's not telling anyone. If she's willing to at least listen to us, then I think it's best if we leave things at that. Some old skeletons are best left buried." Phillip was silent for a moment. "Let me tell you something, friend. You're sitting on a potential powder keg with that woman. She has little enough reason to trust Anglos. You let her know who you are, why you're living here, and you've blown it. She'll take off faster than a wild deer."

"Damn it, Phillip!" Magadan's hands tightened around his glass. He knew the savvy businessman well enough to know Phillip wouldn't be pushed, but dangling a mystery in front of him and then asking him not to push the subject was asking a hell of a lot. "What have you gotten me into with her?"

"It's not me, friend," Phillip grinned. "You're the one who started this business about Kohl. I went along because I figured you were probably the only one with the guts to see it through. I agree, Chela Reola is our best link. I'm not going to say any more about it."

"Why the hell not?"

Phillip frowned. "This isn't getting us anywhere. What's important is trapping Kohl. Have you thought any more about what we talked about earlier?"

The conversation quickly shifted to the possible ramifications and possibility for failure in the plan the two men had devised. Magadan put his businessman's logic to good use by concentrating on the present subject and not dwelling on the points Phillip had raised a few minutes ago. Magadan had been questioning the wisdom of his continued secrecy where Chela was concerned, but Phillip's warning renewed his decision to keep a low profile.

They were discussing the amount of cooperation they could expect from the sheriff and district attorney when the doorbell rang. "I think the young lady is here," Phillip said as he rose. "I wonder if she feels as if she's entering the lion's den."

Magadan was still sitting when Phillip returned, but he rose halfway to his feet before he was aware of what he was doing. What he was aware of was that Chela had exchanged her usual attire for a filmy white sun dress held together by thin straps tied at the shoulder, with a gathered waistline and a softly draping skirt that ended at the knee. The fabric had tiny holes in it—eyelet, Magadan thought it was called—with a white lining under the filmy fabric that teased his senses. Because the top of the garment was loosely gathered, he couldn't be sure whether she was wearing a bra or not, but the thin straps barely any wider than a cord made him believe that the dress was just about all she was wearing. Her tennis shoes had been left somewhere else, and in their place Chela was wearing white sandals.

The contrast between black hair trailing down a slender back and the white summer dress took Magadan's breath away. He couldn't tell whether she was wearing makeup or not but suspected the answer was no. Her cheeks had been given enough color by the sun, and those magnificent doe eyes needed no emphasizing.

"It's been a long time, Chela," Phillip was saying. "The last time we met was at a farm laborers' meeting. You should have worn that dress. No one would have thought to argue with you then."

Chela kept her eyes on Phillip McAndrews and not the man staring at her from the dark, expensive chair. She'd been fighting with herself ever since she stepped out of the bathtub an hour ago. It wasn't that she hated the middle-aged orchardist. The truth was, she rather admired the man's forthright attitude and convictions. If she was a migrant, she would try to find work in McAndrews's orchards. At least he kept the migrant housing on his land in decent repair and paid his workers an honest wage.

"It was a productive meeting," Chela said with more courage than she felt. "A lot of good things came out of it, like the gleaning project. It's about time the pears the pickers didn't get went to feed poor people instead of rotting on the ground."

"They were salvaged because you convinced the orchardists that the project would be adequately supervised. You make an effective speaker for indigents. Look, I'd like to continue exchanging pleasantries with you. You're the best-looking thing to come through this door in a long time, but we have business to discuss."

There was no way Phillip could know what an effort it had taken for her to come here. No way for him to make a connection between her and the grand house farther up the hills. "I don't get to the hills often," she said cautiously, testing the air. "You have a beautiful home."

"It's called keeping up with the Joneses," Phillip snorted. "I swear, every orchardist who ever lived had a home in the east hills. Talk about segregating oneself."

Chela released a long, slow breath. That was a subject she was determined to avoid. "You wanted to talk about something," she said.

"We all need to," Magadan spoke for the first time. "Phillip and I have spent a lot of time working out the details. There were a lot of holes for us to cover."

Chela turned toward Magadan, her hips shifting under the unaccustomed dress. "What am I here for?"

"Why don't you sit down, Chela," Phillip offered. "Can I get you something to drink?"

Chela shook her head and lowered herself slowly into a wooden rocker with a cane backing. She laid her hand along the arms and slid her fingers along the smooth surface. There'd been a chair like this in that house up the hill, but since she'd only been in it once, Chela couldn't be sure how much the two pieces of furniture had in common and how much was a result of her reluctant memory. "Kohl knows me," she said when Phillip was sitting. "He knows what I think of him."

"I've thought of that," Phillip responded. "He's going to be suspicious of you, but if the pot is sweet enough I think it's going to be his undoing. The real question is, would you testify against him in court? Are you committed to seeing this through to the end?"

Chela didn't rush her answer. She realized that her testimony could be crucial in bringing Kohl to justice, but she still had doubts that anything she or the two men in the room could do would actually put an end to his schemes. "We can't leave behind any holes for him to climb through," she said slowly. "This wouldn't be the first time he's been in trouble with the law. He knows his way around the system. He'd get the best lawyer he can afford." Should she tell them that her relationship with Kohl went deeper than they knew? No! She didn't have the words to express that emotion.

"We can afford better," Magadan said. "Phillip and I have discussed this from every possible angle. When he does come to court, and he will, we'll have an airtight case. And there won't be any risk for you."

"I doubt that," Chela replied levelly. "Magadan, I've watched that man operate for years. How do you think he's been able to intimidate the migrants all this time? He backs up his threats."

"He's dealing with uneducated people who won't believe they have any rights. It's going to be different when we set him up."

"And he'll be angrier than he's ever been," Chela pointed out.

"Is that true?" Magadan turned toward Phillip. "Is he capable of violence?"

Phillip nodded, a slow, measured movement. "He's capable of anything. Have you ever seen a wild animal backed into a corner? That's what we'll have on our hands when Kohl realizes he's trapped."

"Then maybe we should forget the whole thing!" Magadan snapped, pushing himself to his feet. "We'll get to him another way. I'm not going to risk her."

Chela stared up at the angry, pacing man. He was deadly serious about what he was saying. None of his performance was calculated to get Chela to do his will. No man had ever come to her defense that way before and Chela responded to his concern. He cared. And because he cared, she believed that Magadan would do everything in his power to keep Kohl away from her. That knowledge gave her courage. It was a simple fact punctuated by the look in Magadan's eyes.

"What is your plan?" she asked calmly, never taking her eyes off Magadan.

He turned on her. "Did you hear me? I'm not taking any risk with your safety."

"I believe it's *my* safety we're discussing," Chela interrupted. "I'm over twenty-one, and no one has ever told me what I can or can't do. I'm the one to make this decision. I want Kohl stopped."

Magadan glared silently at Chela but didn't interrupt when Phillip started talking. Despite the distraction of Magadan's steady gaze, Chela forced herself to concentrate on what the older man was saying. The plan Phillip and Magadan had worked out was simple. It was designed to trap Kohl in one of his oldest and most reliable schemes. Magadan knew a young Mexican living in Mexico City. The man, Ortez Varela, would be willing to return a favor Magadan had done him by participating in the plan. Chela's job would be to convince Kohl that she was willing to pay to have Ortez slipped illegally into the United States. "If we make the pot sweet enough, I think Kohl will take your money and run. Then we'll charge him with theft. Or he'll try to blackmail you into upping the ante. Coercion's a crime."

Disappointed, Chela shook her head. "He's gotten away with cheating people before. If we try to tell a judge we'd paid Kohl to bring an illegal into the country, we're in as much trouble as Kohl is."

"That's where the sting comes in," Magadan entered the conversation for the first time. "Ortez has a green card. He has every right to come here. We just won't tell Kohl that. When we go before the courts, we'll—or you'll—simply state that you paid Kohl to arrange transportation for Ortez to come see you. There's nothing unlawful about that. The DA has been putting bits and pieces of cases together for years. If this works out, it'll simply be the last nail in the coffin. It'll expose him once and for all."

Chela shut her eyes for a moment, focusing her thoughts on what she knew of Kohl. He would do anything for money, and greed would probably get in the way of any caution that would make him suspicious. "I'd have to offer him enough money," she said softly, "otherwise he won't take the risk. And I have to have a good reason to want Ortez here. Kohl will be suspicious of everything I tell him."

"If he thinks you're in love with Ortez, he'll believe what you tell him."

Chela opened her eyes to stare at Magadan. Was there anger and tension in his voice? If Magadan was still angry with her for ignoring his words of concern for her safety, she couldn't help the way she was. She was responding in an all new way toward his concern, but it still didn't alter her independent approach to life. "Maybe," she said slowly.

"Maybe, nothing," Phillip asserted. "You're a single young woman. Kohl would be a fool not to believe you were capable of falling in love. And he knows you make a decent living, could have a savings account. It would make sense to use that money to pay to have your lover brought here."

My lover? A man I've never met? Chela had never thought of herself as an actress, but her pulse quickened at the thought of deceiving Kohl. "How much does Ortez know?" she asked. "What if Kohl gets in touch with him?"

"Ortez will go along with whatever we decide," Magadan said. "Like I said, he owes me a favor. He doesn't have much use for animals who feed on the misery of his countrymen. But do you really think Kohl will contact him? Wouldn't it be more like him to take your money and run?"

Chela shook her head. "Kohl knows how I feel about him. He's not going to take the money if he smells a trap. He won't take anything I say at face value."

"In other words, he doesn't trust you any more than you trust him? It could be dangerous." Anger once again laced Magadan's voice. "Why the hell didn't I think about that more?"

"Because I deliberately left that possibility out of the conversation," Phillip interjected. "I figured the first time you looked at Chela you'd get all protective. I know because she has the same effect on me. But I've known this independent young woman for years. I know what she's capable of."

Chela nodded to acknowledge Phillip's compliment. She'd always had a wary relationship with the older man, but there was a certain respect that existed between the two. "When should I contact Kohl?" she asked.

"Anytime. Joe will make sure you have cash," Phillip said. "Kohl won't take anything but cash. But he isn't going to jump right away. You're right, he's going to sniff this out first."

"I don't want you going out there alone," Magadan said. He'd been leaning against a paneled wall, but now he pushed his body away from it and took a few steps toward where Chela was sitting. "I'm going along."

Chela wanted to laugh at the impossible suggestion, but the narrow slits Magadan's eyes had become stopped her. "I'm sorry," she said softly but firmly. "It won't work unless I'm alone with Kohl. I'm not sure it's going to work anyway, but this is the only way I'll do it."

"I think she has you over a barrel, Magadan," Phillip laughed. "I told you she was an independent lady."

"Then she's a fool. She could get herself killed."

"That isn't how Kohl operates," Chela pointed out despite the distraction of having Magadan looming over her. "He threatens and cheats and lies, but he isn't going to kill anyone."

"No one has ever tried to double-cross him before," Phillip pointed out. "I'm with Magadan on this one. You're going to have to be damn careful."

How do you think I've survived so far? Chela thought, but she kept that to herself. The two men didn't need to hear about the tightrope she walked between two cultures. It wasn't easy to win the trust of migrants even if she had much in common with them, and it wasn't natural for her to walk in Anglo society, but she could do that, too, when necessary. "I'll be careful." Chela waited for a minute and then continued. "Kohl stays out of sight much of the time. I don't know where he is. I'll have to let it be known that I'm looking for him and wait for him to get in touch with me."

"You are one stubborn female." Magadan's fists were clenched, and he was staring even closer than he'd been before. "You keep me informed of everything that's going on. I'm going to give you my phone number. I want yours. I don't want to be out of touch with you at any time."

Giving Magadan her phone number wasn't something Chela did freely, but her survival instinct knew that denying him that request could place her in more danger than either Phillip or the mysterious Magadan knew. The orchardist thought he knew Kohl, but he couldn't know everything the man was capable of. Phillip was an influential orchardist, not a migrant worker.

She was taking chances. It would help tip things in

her direction if she knew Magadan could get in touch
with her at any time. She nodded and then asked for
more information about her mythical Mexican lover.
She would have to be able to describe Ortez, tell Kohl
where he lived, be able to make up some story about
how they'd met and fallen in love. She'd have to explain that love was worth the depletion of her savings
account. Magadan supplied the answers she needed,
but there was no ignoring the anger she sensed sim-
mering in him. He didn't want her doing this.

It had been his idea in the first place. Chela didn't
understand why he was backing off now, showing a
personal concern for her safety. All she knew was that
she was responding to that caring quality in him. She
questioned what she was doing several times, but just
before she stood up, she gave Magadan her address.
"You might need it," was all she would say.

As she turned to leave, Magadan moved with her
and walked out to her Jeep. It wasn't until she was sitting behind the wheel with his hand resting on the rearview mirror that he spoke. "If you get a bad feeling
about this, I want you to tell me. Nothing is worth risking your safety."

Chela turned toward him. "Magadan, this was your
idea in the first place. Don't ever forget that."

"I can't. I just never thought— The sheriff didn't tell
me much about you."

"What did he tell you?"

"That you were competent. That when you sunk
your teeth into something you stuck with it. I thought
that was enough for what I had in mind." His hand left
the rearview mirror and gently touched the length of

hair trailing by her cheek. "Haven't you ever had a man want to take care of you?"

"I don't need a man to take care of me." She should be turning her head to break the contact, but she didn't.

"That's not what I mean," Magadan groaned. "I can't believe you've gone this far in life without meeting a man who wants to be part of your life, to step in when you need a buffer."

Chela blinked her eyes against something vulnerable his words touched. "No one lives in a castle with a moat around it anymore, Magadan, but we all go it alone."

His fingers were playing with her hair, rolling the thick strands together and sliding down the length. "Not everyone does, Chela. A lot of women, the majority in fact, look for someone to share their lives with. It isn't a sign of weakness; it's because they want to belong."

"What about you, Magadan?" she asked, turning the question around. "Why aren't you married?"

Eyes met eyes across the distance framed by a Jeep. "I haven't found the right woman."

Reckless questioning put Chela's thoughts into words. "What is the right woman? What are you looking for?"

"I don't know," he laughed harshly. "Do any of us until we find that special someone? Don't you have any family? Are you really all alone?"

"I told you my mother's dead."

"What about your father? Why isn't he part of your life?"

Chela turned away, the sudden jerk of her head

stretching the hairs Magadan held in his fingers. Slowly, coldly, Chela spoke. "I don't ever want to talk about my father. Do you understand that? That's one question I'm never going to answer."

When Magadan released her hair, Chela started the engine and drove away. She should be thinking about Kohl and how she was going to get in touch with him, but she wasn't. She wasn't even thinking about her father. Instead Chela's thoughts were divided between the task of driving and emotions Magadan had stirred inside her. The man was as much an unknown now as he'd been the first day she saw him. Now, however, her life had been complicated by his presence. He'd stirred up memories she thought she'd buried about her father, but more than that, Magadan was bringing to life strange emotions and longings, such as those that touched her when she saw couples walking together, absorbed in each other.

It all boiled down to a simple fact: Chela didn't want to go home tonight. She didn't want to unlock her door and walk into an empty house. She didn't want to climb into an empty bed.

But Chela slept alone that night as she had most of the nights of her life. In the morning she dressed, had breakfast, and drove to one of the more distant barrios where she'd promised to work with a group of preschoolers. Later in the day she used the excuse of interpreting some English document to go to one of the migrant labor hiring centers. She started slowly, almost tentatively laying the groundwork for the eventual contact with Kohl. She spoke of taking a trip to Mexico several months earlier and falling head over heels in love with a man there. She didn't want to move to Mexico to be with him because she couldn't earn a living there. He wanted to join her in the United States because he'd been able to find only sporadic work with an American business operating in Mexico since the oil industry in Mexico died a sudden death. What distressed Chela the most was Ortez's inability to gain the necessary papers to allow him to cross the border legally. "I have to find a way," Chela finished up to the half dozen listening men. "I have the money, but I'm afraid to try to get him here myself. I'm afraid we'll be stopped. I don't know how to do these things."

Those listening nodded in understanding, but said little. That didn't bother Chela. She was ready to wait until word spread through the underground network of communication that existed in the migrant world. She repeated her story twice more that day and then settled back to wait.

The wait lasted three days. In that time Chela divided her time between the barrios and orchards and assisted in another soccer game. She kept looking around during the game, hoping to see the sturdy frame of the man who'd started her on this adventure, but Magadan didn't show himself. She was home and getting ready for bed Thursday night when he called her.

Chela had been startled to hear her phone ring, but the deep tones on the other end, instead of easing her, only increased her sense of alertness. "I didn't think it would be too wise for me to be seen around you while you're trying to get in touch with Kohl," Magadan explained. "Have you had any luck?"

Chela related her efforts in trying to reach the elusive coyote. "I'm not even sure he's in the valley now. He goes to Mexico whenever there's a need for more workers or the immigration officers have conducted a raid." Chela's voice revealed her bitterness as she continued. "Rob the orchardists of their labor force, and they put out the call for replacements."

"I want you to get in touch with me as soon as he contacts you," Magadan insisted.

"There won't be anything to tell," Chela replied, her lips set against the anger she'd heard in his voice. "He's going to move slowly. He'll want to know a great deal more before he agrees to take my money."

"Does he always work that slowly? That isn't the impression I get of the man."

"That's how he'll be with me. He has no reason to trust me. You know that. He's going to be suspicious." Chela laughed at an ironic thought. "But he's more greedy than he is suspicious. He'll respond to money waved under his nose."

"I just hope you know what you're doing."

"You thought I did when you approached me," Chela pointed out, relieved that she didn't have to face Magadan right now. "What changed your mind?"

"I didn't know you when I got into this. I do now."

"And what have you learned about me, Magadan?" Chela challenged. "Don't you think I'm enough of a woman to do the job?"

Magadan's voice had taken on a slightly husky quality. "You're enough of a woman all right, Chela. But you weren't wearing an old shirt and jeans the other night. I have to think about the feminine side of your nature."

Chela would have laughed except that in a way she barely understood, Magadan had reached a certain nerve that warmed at the thought that he saw her as a woman. "I promise I won't wear a dress again. Will that help?"

"Hardly. Look, I have some things to do before I can go to bed. Just be sure you call me the minute that snake gets in touch with you."

Magadan hung up without giving Chela time to respond. She held the receiver away from her and stared at the silent instrument. When she first heard Magadan's voice, she'd acknowledged a rush of warmth that spread quickly through her body, but now she only felt confused and a little hurt. What possessed the man to go from giving her a compliment to being abrupt in the space of a single breath? If he was regretting the necessity of their having to deal with each other, Chela was sorry, but it was too late. Now that she knew she had the backing of McAndrews and Magadan, she was determined to snare Kohl in the trap they'd set for him. She'd cut her teeth on rising to challenges, succeeding despite practically having to raise herself. As Chela replaced the receiver, she couldn't help asking if she'd enjoy becoming a secret agent. Hardly, she admitted. There was a much deeper satisfaction in exposing migrant children to an education, improving the lives of their parents. But a little adventure slipped into one's life did add a certain spice to it.

At least that was the way she could feel now since she hadn't actually had to come face to face with Kohl.

For the third night in a row, Chela's sleep was filled with disturbing dreams that eluded her in the morning.

All she knew was that she rose feeling vaguely discontented and aching for something that had yet to touch her life. She tried to tell herself that her mood came from not knowing when, if at all, she would hear from Kohl. But as she faced herself in the bathroom mirror, her tired eyes told her that wasn't what made sleep elusive.

By the time she'd finished working that day and pulled back into her driveway, Chela felt as tired as she knew her eyes looked. The temperature had reached more than one hundred degrees, sapping her mind and body. She'd managed to keep alive the story of her Mexican lover but wasn't sure how convincing her story was. Chela had never had what she could call a lover. She didn't know what words women used when they spoke of men who brought them to life, who ruled their hearts and thoughts and bodies. She wondered if hers lacked a ring of conviction and if Kohl would be able to see through her ruse. And why did she find herself thinking of Magadan during the odd moments when she didn't have to concentrate on a child's English?

There was no denying it. Until Chela managed to get a decent night's sleep, she wasn't going to be able to take an objective look at her performance. She was almost too tired to prepare dinner and settled for a bowl of soup. Even a bath seemed too much of an effort. She was settled on a couch with the evening paper, wearing nothing but a cool, summery bathrobe, when someone knocked at her front door.

For a moment she didn't move. Some instinct warned her that the time for action had come. At length, despite the tension that had surged through her at the knock, Chela stood up and walked to the door.

Ray Kohl stood just outside.

Chela clamped down hard on her lower lip to stifle the gasp that rose in her throat. She also forced her hands to remain on the door and not clutch her bathrobe. "What are you doing here?" was the best she could manage.

"Talk, Chela. You and I have things to talk about."

Slowly, deliberately, Chela backed up and let Kohl in. Any hesitancy, any show of fear on her part now could destroy what she was trying to accomplish. She had to act as if she wanted to talk to Kohl. She nodded toward the couch she'd vacated and waited for the hard-eyed man to sit down. She chose her favorite chair near the wood stove and sat down herself, taking comfort in the fact that her robe was made of an opaque fabric that hid the fact that she wore nothing under it. She pushed her hair back from her face and waited for Kohl to make the first move.

Kohl's eyes were roaming slowly and yet intensely around the room. Sitting, he didn't seem to be large enough to wield the power she knew he was capable of. But his hands and feet were massive in comparison to the rest of his wiry frame, and that lent credibility to his reputation. His dark hair looked as if it hadn't been washed in weeks, and yet his clothes were so new that they probably hadn't been laundered yet. His face showed the effects of both exposure to hours of sunlight and nights spent in smoke-filled bars.

"So Chela Reola has a love."

Chapter Five

Chela took several deep breaths to calm herself before speaking. She wasn't physically afraid of Kohl. That wasn't the way the man operated, at least not with people who might charge him with anything that could stick. But Kohl hadn't lasted in his career as long as he had without being a cagey judge of character. The slightest slip, the most minute uncertainty on Chela's part, and he would see through her.

"Word travels fast in the orchards," she said, aware that his eyes were divided between her face and hands. "You heard."

"I heard a story that Chela Reola has found herself a Mexican lover. A man who can't leave Mexico. But Chela Reola isn't a woman who gives herself readily to any man. True, more like a Mexican than an Anglo, but I've yet to see your heart rule your head."

"It's true." Chela deliberately dropped her eyes and stared at her hands. Kohl thrived on feeling that he was in control. All right. She'd play the submissive role. "I didn't mean for it to happen. I flew to Mexico in May to see some of my mother's family. While there I met Ortez Varela."

"A laborer? Chela has given herself to a laborer?"

Chela bristled at the insinuation that her romance was no more than physical. Still she held her temper in check. "Ortez is no laborer. He went to the university," she continued proudly. "He worked in the oil fields, but that's gone now. There's very little work for him." She allowed a measure of bitterness to enter her voice. "There's unemployment everywhere. He wants to leave, but he's made enemies with the government and they won't give him a green card because of his political views."

"You could send him money," Kohl challenged. "It doesn't take a man with two eyes to see that you don't spend your salary on clothing."

Chela cringed at the personal reference but refused to let it show in her voice. Instead she brought her head up slowly and faced the man. It took all the acting ability she was capable of, but she continued. "I don't want him in Mexico, living off a woman. I want Ortez here with me. A man has to work to have pride. I can get him that work here."

"But you can't get him here legally. For once Chela Reola can't have what she wants."

The jab, Chela knew, was designed to test her. For a moment she wasn't sure she'd be able to pull off her act any longer. The threads of her past were all too well-known to Kohl, only Kohl. "I never saw a penny of my father's money," Chela said levelly, calmly, the anger held firmly inside. "I've had to work for everything

I've gotten. What I have in the bank didn't come easy.''

"Do you want me to cry for you, Chela?" Kohl asked, leaning forward so that his small eyes reached further inside than Chela wanted. "In this world it's every man for himself. I know what you think of me. And you know I have no use for you—at least no use that would be served out of bed. We have too much in common, Chela. Your father is going to bind us together for as long as either of us lives."

"I don't want to talk about that!" What had possessed her father to point out his daughter to Kohl? Of course he was going to try to use that to his advantage. Chela rose halfway to her feet before she could stop herself. This wasn't the direction the conversation needed to go. He was only testing her by bringing up her father's name and the cruel past. Slowly, deliberately, Chela settled back in her chair and stared unblinking at Kohl until she'd regained control over her emotions. "You're right," she said finally. "We have too much in common. But because we do, I know what you're capable of. I have money."

"So I've heard." Kohl was smiling, his yellowed teeth exposed by dry lips. "That's why I'm here. You have a need; I know how to provide the service. But it will cost you."

"More than it would someone else who needs you, isn't that so?" Chela asked boldly.

"You know me well, as I know you. Yes, if I bring Ortez to you, it will cost you much more than my usual fee."

Chela stifled a laugh. Usual fee? Kohl thought of

spiriting Mexicans across the border as if it was no more than a service he performed for the orchardists he had contracts with. But wasn't that what a coyote was? Kohl was simply a businessman who operated outside the law. "How much?"

"That, my sweet lady, depends on many things." He paused, laced his fingers together, and stared at Chela the way a vulture would stare at a rabbit caught in a trap. "For certain services performed I would lower my fee."

Chela wasn't shocked. She'd known from the beginning that he would use this approach. In addition to acting as a coyote, Kohl occasionally provided women for lonely men. Nothing would give him a greater sense of victory than having her in his stable or, perhaps more than that, keeping her for himself. The thought made Chela want to gag, but because she'd known the moment would come sometime during their meeting, she was able to deal with it without becoming physically ill. "Name your fee, Kohl," she said, her voice so low it was almost a growl. "There will be no compromises."

"Don't be so sure, my wild one. We all have our price, we all have our breaking points. I could involve your father in this."

Chela felt bile rising in her throat. Every instinct aimed at survival screamed at her to flee the room and the terrible threat Kohl was holding over her. Her father! Was the man back in the area? Would he confront her if Kohl asked him to? What—what if Magadan learned who her father was?

Only one thought kept Chela from burying her nails

in the calculating face sitting across from her. Kohl succeeded because he believed in the power of intimidation. What if she called his bluff and in the end it was she who succeeded? He would be behind bars, and Chela would no longer have to fear the man who was her link with her father. "If I ever see my father again, you'll never see a penny of the money I have set aside to bring Ortez here."

Kohl didn't reply right away. Instead the small eyes seemed to glaze over as if he was concentrating on turning the thought around and around in his mind. Finally, "You don't bluff, Chela. If anything, you're too honest. I could walk out that door. You'd never see Ortez again."

Chela bit her lip to keep from smiling. She'd won this round! "I don't want to live in Mexico, but I would if that was the only way Ortez and I could be together. I'm offering you more money than you see in a month for a few days' work," she said calmly. "You'd be a fool to turn it down."

"We'll see who's the fool, Chela. You'll understand if I find it hard to believe that you've come running to me for help simply because you want to crawl into some man's bed." Kohl pushed against the arm of the couch and got to his feet. "Passion must learn patience. I have some questions I want answered before I take your money. I want to know how to get in touch with this Ortez. If I decide you're telling me the truth, I'll get in touch with you again."

"I didn't expect it to be any different." Chela rose, too, walked over to the telephone, and picked up the piece of paper with the address Magadan had given her. "Ortez will be expecting to hear from you."

"Maybe. And maybe he won't be expecting the questions I ask him." Kohl took the paper. Before Chela could draw her hand away, he grabbed her wrist with his oversized fingers and pulled her toward him. Chela could smell the stale whiskey on his breath as he leaned toward her. "I don't make idle threats, Chela. You'll regret it if you aren't being honest with me."

Chela willed herself not to let him know how repulsed she was. Courage was one of the few things he respected. "I'm not a frightened illegal," she said. "Touch me and I'll go to the police."

"Maybe. Maybe. There's one thing you better not forget, Chela. I know who your father is. Your employers don't. The migrants who trust you don't. You'd be an outcast if they were to find out that your father is—"

"Stop it!" Had she kept enough of the hysteria she felt out of her voice so he wouldn't guess how close to the edge he'd brought her? "I'm telling you the truth," she went on desperately. "Talk to Ortez. All I want is him here with me. I'm willing to pay for it."

"Oh, yes, Chela Reola." Kohl pulled her ever closer to his yellow teeth. "You'll pay. In every way I want you to." He was smiling as he fastened his left hand around her free arm and pressed his body against hers.

Chela stumbled backward, animal instinct stripping her of every rational thought. She'd told herself that Kohl was capable of using this approach on her, but the actuality of it happening was almost more than she could handle. "Get out of here! Get out, or you'll be sorry you were ever born."

Kohl didn't reply until he had her backed against the living-room wall. He pressed his legs against hers, his mouth so close that she was forced to throw her head backward until her head touched the wall. "Don't threaten me, Chela, or you'll be sorry. You cherish your precious freedom. How would you like to have no life beyond what I decide for you? How would you like to live your days in a little room and your nights in the arms of whatever men I bring to you?"

An animallike sob crawled its way up Chela's throat, but she refused to give it life. Kohl was capable of that; he was capable of anything. But she wasn't a helpless woman at his mercy. She had the law on her side, Magadan waiting for her call. "Don't threaten me either," she managed in the low growl that had escaped her lips before. "I'd die before I'd let that happen to me."

"It could come to that." He grinned. "There's just one thing I want you to understand, Chela. No one double-crosses me, no one. I'm not a stupid man who stops thinking simply because someone waves money at me. I don't trust you any more than you trust me. If you're lying to me...." He left unsaid what his punishing fingers and legs were telegraphing.

Kohl didn't give her time to answer. The thin lips that had been so close came even closer, teasing, challenging. Chela tried to turn her head to one side, but his mouth followed hers. He imprisoned her against the wall, capturing her mouth, teeth pressing cruelly against the soft flesh.

Chela closed her eyes in a desperate attempt to fight the revulsion surging through her body. The urge to attack, to punish, was so strong that it almost overwhelmed her. But she knew what he was capable of if he became angry enough. She had to submit to his repulsive kiss, play the hated passive role. One wrong move on her part, and she would lose the chance she had of putting the revolting little coyote out of business.

The kiss went on until Chela thought she would scream, but finally he gave her a small measure of freedom. "I'll be back," Kohl promised, his fingers digging into her wrists. "When I have my answers, then we'll know whether we'll be dealing in money or your freedom."

He was gone, the door slamming behind him. Chela didn't move until she heard his car drive away. She tried to push herself away from the wall but realized that her legs could barely support her. As she stumbled to the couch, she found herself irrationally blaming Magadan and Phillip McAndrews. They were the ones who'd gotten her into this! It was their fault that Kohl was threatening her with her father!

The thought lasted only until Chela had rid her lips of the residue of Kohl's kiss, if it could be considered a kiss. She'd known what she was letting herself in for when she agreed to work with Magadan. It wasn't his fault that he didn't know of the evil thread that tied her to Kohl.

And he'd never know. The part of the past that included her father was something she'd fought to bury for years. Word of it would never willingly pass her lips.

Chela sank deeper into her favorite rocking chair until she was resting her head against the back. She closed her eyes, fought off what she could of the emotions assaulting her as a result of Kohl's visit. Slowly her breathing returned to normal. It was impossible to return to the calm she'd known before he walked in the door, but at least now she could think again. Kohl had contacted her. Magadan would want to know that.

As she made her way to the phone and picked up the receiver, Chela refused to let herself admit how much it would mean to hear Magadan's voice. It wasn't until she heard his voice that she acknowledged the rush of warmth that spread through her. "Kohl just left," she said in a voice she didn't recognize.

"Are you all right? You don't sound so good."

A deep breath. Good. Now she could go on. "He hates me. The meeting wasn't pleasant."

"And that's all you want to tell me, isn't it?" Magadan asked. "Don't you move. I'm coming right over."

"No! You don't have to—"

"I'll be there in ten minutes if I don't spot Kohl. I'll leave my truck up the road and walk through the field." He hung up before she could respond.

Chela went into the bathroom and splashed cold water on her face. She gripped the towel tightly to still the unaccustomed trembling in her fingers and focused on the dark eyes staring back at her in the mirror. They were larger than usual with a vulnerable, wounded look she hated. What her father had done to her and her mother was something she hadn't been able to forgive...or forget. Most of the time the past rested deep in her subconscious, but Kohl had given the memories freedom. She knew it would be that way. She just hadn't known that her eyes would give the memories away.

Don't touch me Magadan, she warned silently. *Don't*

ask questions I don't want to answer. You have your se-
crets. Let me have mine.

By the time she heard Magadan's truck pull into her
driveway, Chela believed she'd regained enough self-
control to be able to face him. What she didn't expect
was to have him push open the door without knocking.
He filled the opening, blinking to make out his surroundings in the dimly lit room. "Are you all right?"
he asked as he closed the door behind him.

"Of course." She forced a shaky laugh and retreated
to her rocker. "Kohl doesn't have much use for me.
The feeling is mutual."

"I want to know everything that happened. Is he going to take the bait?"

It wasn't the question Chela expected. She'd been
hoping, despite herself, that he'd show more concern
than he was. But in truth this was better. She could
maintain control as long as he stood across from her
and let his eyes take in her living room.

"I don't know," she answered, when at length he
stopped his exploration, sat down, and his eyes settled
back on her. "He wants to get in touch with Ortez
first."

"He's no fool. Phillip told me he wouldn't be easy to
trap. What did he say to you?"

"Nothing." Chela bit her lower lip. She hadn't
meant to answer so quickly. "Nothing I didn't expect,"
she amended. Magadan's hair was disheveled as if he'd
been interrupted when the phone rang and hadn't
taken time to look at himself in the mirror before coming here. For an instant a thought filled Chela. Perhaps
he had been with a woman.

"Sorry," he was saying. "That's not good enough. Look, it's my money I'm putting up for this little scheme. I'm the one who made the contacts with Ortez. I deserve more of an answer than that."

Chela stared at Magadan. Did she just imagine it, or had his eyes flickered downward for a moment, recording her attire? He was a businessman. It was a businessman's question. "I'm the one taking the risks," she pointed out sharply. "I have to handle this the way I feel is best."

"By being closemouthed? Damn it, Chela, that's not what our agreement was."

"Agreement? Do you want to sign a contract?" Agitated, Chela pushed a nonexistent strand of hair out of her eyes.

Magadan was staring at her hand. He didn't speak as he rose to his feet and came to stand over her. She tried to pull her hand away, but he took it and held it up near the lamp beside the recliner. Chela turned to see what Magadan was staring at. That was when she noticed the marks left by Kohl's punishing fingers. "He did that," Magadan said. It wasn't a question.

Chela tried unsuccessfully to pull away. "It doesn't matter. I expected it. That's the way he operates."

"Not with you he doesn't. The bastard!"

Were those words of protection Magadan was using? Because she'd never heard them before, Chela couldn't answer her own question. "It's a part of the game we're playing, Magadan," Chela replied calmly, hiding the turmoil inside. "Kohl has to believe he's in control of the situation. That's the way he operates. You should know that by now. That's the only thing he understands. When he believes he has me where he wants me, he'll go for the prize we're offering."

"Where he wants you?" Magadan released her hand, but instead of returning to his seat, he knelt beside her recliner. "There's something you aren't telling me."

"Maybe." Chela willed herself not to move, meeting his eyes much more willingly than she'd met the slimy coyote's.

"But if it's something Kohl can use against you—"

"I'm not afraid of him." Was that the truth?

"You should be. Damn it, Chela. I can't believe the gall of the man. He had no right hurting you the way he did. Was that all you were wearing?"

Chela glanced down at her robe. Her breasts were faintly outlined under the soft fabric. "Kohl doesn't want me," she said softly. "He knows I hate him too much to allow that to happen."

"Why?"

Chela tossed her hair back, eyes flashing a warning. "That, Magadan, is none of your business."

"Don't be so sure." Again Magadan was on his feet. This time he was pacing, his emotions seemingly too much for the confines of the room. Because Chela seldom had a man in her house, she was mesmerized by the way Magadan fit in it. She'd always thought of the house as a mirror of what she was, private, basic. A man like Magadan shouldn't look at home in a house with hardwood floors, rough-cut paneling, oil paintings of outdoor scenes, and Mexican blankets thrown over the backs of furniture. But he did fit. Tonight he was in jeans and a T-shirt, as if he'd casually thrown off the trappings of success she'd seen him in earlier. His tennis shoes made little noise on the solid floor.

He turned on her. "Do you know what I wish? I wish you were a big truck driver of a woman with cold, calculating eyes. If I'd known the sheriff was talking about a creature with eyes like a wild deer and a body made for a man to touch—" Magadan ran a hand roughly over his forehead. "You're complicating my life in a way I never thought would happen."

For a moment Chela couldn't trust herself to speak. Those were gentle words, words capable of touching her heart, but there were too many barriers between them. Kohl had reminded her of who she was. "Don't do this, Magadan," she whispered. "We have a business arrangement. It can't go any further than that."

"Magadan?" He spat out the word. "Can't you call me Joe?"

Chela kept her eyes on the man pacing in the confines of her room. A deer he'd called her. Did he have any idea how much animal was in him? Animals react to one another on a primitive basis. Tonight Chela was a primitive creature. Her words came hard. "You said that everyone calls you Magadan. Why should I be different?"

"I don't know." He laughed bitterly. "Maybe because I'm tired of the distance inherent in the word. Don't you ever want to get close to someone, trust them completely?"

Of course, I do, Chela admitted to herself. *Do you have any idea how it's been for me since my mother died?* "Trust takes a long time, Magadan," she whispered. "You and I haven't reached that point yet."

"Then maybe it's time we started." He stopped his pacing, whirled toward her so quickly that his shoes squealed a protest. "I want to know everything that happened with Kohl, how he put those marks on you."

Chela didn't dare take her eyes off the man dominating the room. Whether she wanted it or not, Magadan was putting his mark on her. The difference was that his impact didn't show physically. She drew in air through flared nostrils and started. "I can't tell you everything, Magadan. Not yet, and maybe not ever. But Kohl and I go back a long way. He knows... things about me. He isn't going to jump into anything that I'm a part of; he has no reason to trust me. Those marks are his way of making sure I don't forget that."

Chela went on. She told Magadan that she'd known Kohl since she was a child and he a teenager, already a pro in the darker ways of making money. She skirted around the question of why or how their paths first crossed, just that no love had ever been lost between the two. "It's funny in a way," she wound up. "I can't help but admire the man. I don't know anyone else who has been on the wrong side of the law all his life and managed to elude it so long." Her voice dropped to a whisper. "Most lawbreakers trip themselves up sooner or later. They have to pay the price." And so do those around them, she added silently.

"So now we wait." Magadan sighed. He sank into the couch Kohl had used, his eyes narrowing as if seeking a private conversation with himself.

"That's all we can do," Chela acknowledged, grateful that he wasn't kneeling next to her anymore. They were back to talking business. Good, that was what she could handle. "He'll be back. He smells easy money."

"We can't allow a slipup. I want him...now."

"Maybe you'll get him," Chela admitted, but with reservations. "Don't forget, he's played this game longer than either of us."

"I'll get him. Look, have you had dinner?"

"What? Yes. I was getting ready for bed when he came."

Magadan leaned forward. "Will you be able to sleep?"

Although her muscles ached, Chela knew sleep would probably never come tonight. "I've had sleepless nights before," she admitted. "Another won't kill me."

"Maybe. But there's no reason why you should do it alone."

What was he suggesting? "I sleep alone, Magadan," she whispered.

"That's not what I meant. When you and I go to bed, Chela, it'll be because both of us want it, not because I'm bigger and stronger than you. Look, why don't you change and I'll take you out for some ice cream."

Ice cream—after what she'd been through tonight? Chela thought back to her bland bowl of soup and realized that ice cream was what she wanted more than anything else she could think of. Maybe a cone would cool her inflamed emotions. "That's the best idea I've heard all day," she said quickly, in an effort to take the conversation beyond bedroom talk. "I—do you really want to do that?"

"I really want to buy you the biggest sundae they

have. Why don't you put on that white sun dress you were wearing the other day?"

Chela rose and braced herself on legs that were slow to do her bidding. She left Magadan and went into her bedroom. He had noticed the difference in her appearance. That wasn't all Chela was thinking about as she slipped out of her robe and reached for the only true touch of femininity in her wardrobe.

Chela turned quickly at the sound of the door opening. She had the dress in her hands, but she was wearing nothing. Her bathrobe lay on the floor. Magadan came all the way into the room and leaned on the doorjamb. "Tell me to leave and I will," he said softly.

She should tell him to get out of her room, scream at him that she was entitled to some measure of privacy. But she didn't. As she reached into her dresser for a pair of panties, Chela acknowledged the caress of his eyes searching her body. She dropped the dress on her bed and stepped into her panties, pulling nylon over the paler flesh untouched by the sun. She straightened, knowing that he had a clear view of her high, pointed breasts with their dark tips.

It wasn't until she'd slipped the eyelet fabric over her head and was adjusting the waistline that Magadan spoke. "You aren't as dark as I thought you were. The sun has left its mark on most of you, but not all."

"I had an Anglo father, remember. You're the one who reminded me of that."

"I don't know why you should be ashamed of that." Magadan leaned over and then handed her her sandals. "The two cultures are a perfect blend on you."

"Hardly." Chela laughed bitterly. "You don't know

my father." She took a deep breath. "Forget I said that."

"How can I forget? All I know about you is that you were a child when your mother died. I take it your parents weren't living together and your father didn't lift a finger when you were left alone. Did he know your mother had died?"

Chela reached up to adjust the dress straps, but her fingers had lost all feeling. "He knew. He learned through the grapevine that exists in the orchards. But why should he care? He'd left my mother before I was born."

"What happened then?"

Chela hadn't been asked that question enough times to be able to answer it easily. "A social worker came and took me to a shelter home. Some months later they found an older couple willing to civilize a dirty little girl who couldn't even speak English. Mr. and Mrs. Roberts saw the need to civilize me as a religious duty. They fed me, taught me to sit silently at the dinner table." Chela tossed her head back defiantly, shaking off the pain. "I was given the material things a child needs. They didn't want me to have any contact with Mexicans, but Mexicans were the only friends I had at school. I went to their houses, learned to laugh there." Chela closed her eyes. "That's why my life is the way it is now. I'm comfortable in a barrio, not surrounded by Anglos."

"The Robertses didn't love you?"

Chela strangled a sob. No! That was hiding, she reminded herself. She wasn't going to let it color today. "They were doing their duty. No one asked them to do anything more."

Chela was still strapping on her sandals when Magadan walked over to her dresser and picked up her hairbrush. She straightened when he started running the brush through her rich hair. For a moment Chela thought about taking the brush from him, but stopped herself before she could put an end to what had quickly become a very sensual experience. Magadan was slowly, gently, brushing the tangles out of her hair, his free hand smoothing down the heavy length. His fingers touched her cheeks, ears, and neck at the same time. Chela tried to stand motionless as Magadan worked on her, but her body flushed and then quivered slightly as his face came closer to hers, his eyes dark and deep.

"You have beautiful hair," he said in a ragged voice. "I hope you never cut it."

She started to say something about split ends that developed if she didn't keep it trimmed, but the words were too everyday for what she was experiencing. Magadan was still drawing the brush through her hair, although it now lay smooth and sleek around her shoulders. There was no need for him to continue doing what he was, but she didn't tell him that. Chela would be content if Magadan never stopped his caressing gestures.

When she was at the point where she wasn't sure she would be able to retain her balance without grabbing him for support, Magadan dropped the brush on the bed, took both her hair and her shoulders in his hands and turned her around so their bodies were only inches apart. "I've wanted to brush your hair since the first day I saw you," he said in that same ragged voice.

Chela thought about never having had a man stroke

her hair before and admitting she'd desperately needed that brand of contact, but she couldn't speak. Magadan was all she could see in the room, the only presence she was aware of. She felt her body being pulled closer and closer to his as if he were a magnet and she the metal filings caught in its grip.

His lips were on hers before she had to admit that she was offering hers to him. The touch was a soft caress and yet spoke of a strength that rocked her entire body. Chela moaned, tears filling her eyes as she surrendered to the emotions surging between them. She was being kissed by Joe Magadan, a man she'd been physically aware of from the moment she first saw him staring at her in an orchard. Given the determination of the man, his lips were softer than she thought they'd be. She took that knowledge and locked it deep inside her. It made the man even more complex than she was; she welcomed that complexity.

Magadan's hands left her shoulders and pressed against her back, pulling her close to him with a determination that both frightened and thrilled her. "When we go to bed together," Magadan had said. If he wanted her tonight, there was no way she'd be able to fight him off. His power over her was that great.

Chela no longer tried to keep her eyes open. She wanted to block off the world, even Magadan's image. She needed, without thinking about it, to experience this kiss, this embrace with no outside distractions. She was no longer aware of eyelet fabric brushing against legs unaccustomed to a skirt, sandal straps over her ankle. What she was aware of was her breasts being flattened against Magadan's chest, the deep rhythm of his breathing that became her rhythm as well. Her arms found his neck and gave her the support her strangely weakened body needed. She felt the corded muscles along the side of his neck and thought, fleetingly, that they didn't feel like the muscles of a businessman who spent his life at a desk.

Magadan's hands were sliding slowly down her back. They found her waist and the swell of the upper part of her buttocks. His hands stopped there, but they were pressing against her until she was forced to arch her body toward him. Even that more intimate contact wasn't something Chela wanted to fight. In her present state, she might have been willing to do anything this man wanted her to do.

Why she'd never felt this way before, why she should be so willing to surrender her separate self to him, were questions that would have to wait for saner moments. All Chela knew now was that she needed to feel the pressure of Magadan against her, a pressure that bordered on the painful but was eased because of the gentle touch of his lips.

When her hands started to ache from having to reach so high, Chela let them slip down Magadan's shoulders until she was clinging to his upper arms. She couldn't completely spread her fingers across the expanse of his arms, and that bothered her. She wanted more control over this man, wanted to feel that she could draw him to her as surely as he'd drawn her to him.

"Are you sure you want ice cream?" Magadan asked, tearing his lips from hers. His mouth found the side of her neck, lips and teeth and tongue exploring the long, taut line of her neck as Chela, breathing deeply, arched her body to give him greater access to her flesh.

I can stop anytime, she told herself, *anytime.* But that moment didn't seem to want to come. It wasn't until his hands left her hips and started to seek her breasts that Chela took a shuddering breath and pulled away. "Strawberry sundae, with nuts," were the only words she could manage.

"You're sure?" Had his voice always sounded that far away or was he having trouble speaking himself?

"I'm sure." Another deep breath for composure and a firm shove of her hands against Magadan's chest accompanied her statement. Now Chela was free. "You said something about our going to bed when we both want it. That hasn't happened yet."

Chapter Six

Once they were in Magadan's truck, Chela didn't pay attention to where they were going. She knew they were heading toward the main part of town, but driving and making decisions about where they were going was Magadan's responsibility. She trusted him; she didn't even question that trust. Chela was content to sit with her head resting against the backrest, lazy eyes vaguely aware of the interplay of neon lights and night sky passing by them. The hot breeze coming in the open window brushed Chela's cheeks, adding to the heat that remained in her body.

Chela was glad Magadan didn't feel a need to fill the truck's interior with talk. She had things to talk about that had to do with emotion, and hunger, and wanting, stirring inside her that had never before seen the light of life.

Until those moments in her bedroom, Chela hadn't thought about a hunger that had to be satisfied. Surrendering herself to a man hadn't happened yet. She had never found a man she wanted to get that close to, but more than that, until Joe Magadan entered her life, she hadn't been challenged to take the risk of letting a man touch her heart.

Now the risk, the challenge, was sitting next to her. His intense eyes were on the road, his mouth a tight line, his knuckles white on the steering wheel. His body language told her that he was wrestling with something that couldn't be translated into words, but Chela didn't have the emotional energy to wonder about the thoughts going through his mind. She had enough to do looking deep into her heart and trying to understand what was happening to it.

Chela had lived wondering if she'd always be alone, that losing her mother and feeling nothing for her father would be the overriding emotions in her life. It wasn't until this night that Chela started to experience another emotion. She wanted to truly get to know another human being and make him part of her life.

"I think it's going to be a sundae, all right." Magadan broke into her reverie in a voice that was so everyday it was a slap to Chela's emotions. "I've got a real weakness for chocolate syrup. I know just the place."

Chela pulled back and matched, at least on the outside, his mood. "I still want strawberry."

Magadan laughed and touched her lightly on the shoulder. "Good. I went with a woman once who was always on a diet. We never got to go anywhere fun to eat."

Chela didn't want to hear about another woman. "Are you sure you can afford this?" she asked, amazed at her ability to keep the conversation light. "I'm not a cheap date."

"If I wanted a cheap date, I wouldn't be with you.

Do you know what I was thinking about the other day?" The teasing had gone out of Magadan's voice. "I'd like to take you out to the most expensive restaurant in town. I want to order lobster and a carafe of wine and maybe take you dancing afterward."

"Why?"

"Have you ever done that before?"

Chela forced a laugh. "You know I haven't. I don't have anything to wear."

"That's why I want to take you to that restaurant. Indulge me. I want to see you pampered. I want to see you in a dress that would knock everyone's eyes out and have you try a vintage wine and lobster with drawn butter."

Chela sighed. She'd never wanted that before, but somehow tonight she did. "Do you think I'd like lobster?"

"There's only one way to find out. We're going to do that soon."

"But I don't have a knock-out dress."

"I'll buy you one. But first"—Magadan slowed and then pulled into the parking lot of an ice-cream shop—"two sundaes, chocolate and strawberry."

Chela was at the public park helping Jeff Cline coach the soccer team through another game, grateful for the diversion. For the first time since she'd last seen Magadan three days ago, she had something else to think about.

"I think the team would like to see the big roller back again," Jeff admitted after an unsuccessful attempt to get the boys to listen to what he and Chela were trying to tell them. "It isn't often someone comes around to treat the team like that. Have you heard anything more from him?"

Chela frowned. She wanted to talk about soccer, not about a man with the power to make her question everything she'd come to believe about herself. She didn't want to remember a silent drive home and a light kiss that didn't go far enough. "A little," she admitted.

"Yeah? Who is he? He acts as if he has the world by the tail. What is he, a lawyer, a banker?"

"I don't know. He won't tell me that about himself."

"Sounds mysterious. You don't think he'd like to adopt a starving college student, do you? He might have some extra money he doesn't know what to do with."

"I don't know about that," Chela admitted before turning the conversation back to soccer. And yet even when her team scored another goal, Chela found it impossible to shake off the sudden depressed mood that had settled over her. She didn't know nearly enough about Magadan. He was putting up the money needed to snare Kohl, and yet she had no idea where that money was coming from. It wasn't fair! He knew where she lived, how she supported herself, that her mother was dead, that she'd been raised by people who had remained strangers to her. Why wouldn't he tell her anything about himself?

When the game was over, Chela and Jeff managed to scrape together enough money between the two of them to buy the boys a small soft drink apiece, but it wasn't the same thing. They obviously wanted the stranger with the fat pocketbook to come back. "Now I'm going to have to eat beans for a week to make up for what I spent tonight," Jeff complained as they were carrying the soccer gear to his battered old car. "I hope those characters appreciate my sacrifice. I also hope your mysterious friend realizes that he's spoiled the team and we're having to live with the consequences."

"I don't know what he realizes," Chela said as Jeff was getting into his car. She stepped back, holding her breath as blue smoke billowed out from the tail pipe, and then waved the college student off. If only Magadan was more like Jeff. Jeff took college and coaching and pinching pennies seriously, and yet he bounced through life with an openness that Chela had been drawn to from the first day she met the young man. There probably wasn't anything about Jeff that he wouldn't tell her if she asked.

The difference was she didn't want to know everything about Jeff.

Chela was climbing into her Jeep when the truck with its oversized tires pulled in front of her vehicle and stopped inches away, making it impossible for her to leave. She waited as Magadan cut his engine and walked over to her.

"I missed the game." He pointed back toward his truck. "I bought a few treats for the boys. Do you think we can get the stuff to them?"

"They have another game on Wednesday," Chela supplied. Then, "You don't have to do that."

"I know. I just like spending money on people I like. Do you have time to shop for that dress we were talking about?"

"What?" Chela glanced down at herself. There were grass stains on her knees, her tennis shoes were dusty, and she knew her hair was no longer the smooth length Magadan had caressed the other night. "I can't. And—Magadan, I can't let you do something like that for me."

"Why?" His eyes echoed the challenge in his voice.

"Because I've never had anyone buy something for me like that."

Magadan shook his head. "And you're a liberated woman who wouldn't think of letting a man buy a trinket for her. What would that be—compromising yourself?"

"I don't know. I just can't let you do that." Why was it so hard for her to organize her thoughts?

"Is that so? Well, maybe I have a say in that. What if I just show up one day with a dress under my arm? You'd have to accept it gracefully, even if it isn't what you want. It'd be a lot better if we went shopping together."

"I can't." Chela stuck out her stained leg for emphasis. "They won't let me try on a dress looking like this."

"You have a point. Tomorrow. I'll pick you up at your place about five."

"I don't want you to," she objected. "I don't need a dress like you're talking about."

"How do you know what kind of dress I'm thinking of? Besides, I'm not buying a lobster dinner for someone looking the way you do right now. Five. At your place." Magadan turned around and started back toward his truck. Chela started to open her mouth but changed the words as they came out. "It's good to see you," she said softly instead. "I didn't expect—"

"That's me," he threw over his shoulder. "Mysterious."

At first Chela wasn't going to let Magadan take her shopping for a dress she didn't need. Then she was, because, right or wrong, she had always wondered what it would be like to have one truly exquisite dress. Magadan shouldn't pay for her clothes, she kept telling herself. But why not? He wanted to do it. Maybe they'd never have that expensive dinner. Maybe this was all some joke he was pulling on her.

Despite her conflicting emotions, Chela hurried through her afternoon lessons the next day and came home to clean up before Magadan was due to arrive. She decided against the white eyelet dress, thinking that he deserved to see something else on her. She grew desperate rummaging through her sparse belongings. At last she grabbed the blazer, blouse, and straight skirt she'd bought for when she had to meet with the school officials. The confining fabric around her thighs and long sleeves over arms used to being free felt wrong, but Chela had nothing else to wear. As she glanced at herself in what passed for a mirror in her bathroom, she realized that her hair was all wrong for the outfit. She should have it piled up in some kind of sophisticated style, but doing sophisticated things with her hair was a skill she had never learned.

Why was she putting herself through this? Chela asked herself. She didn't belong in a dress shop looking for a dress that was a world removed from migrant life.

The knock on the door came right at five. Chela took a shaky breath, tried to concentrate on taking short steps that wouldn't strain the narrow skirt, and opened the door.

Magadan was wearing jeans and a short-sleeve rugby shirt with the two neckline buttons opened. He glanced at Chela's outfit and slowly shook his head. "You remind me of how I felt when I was a boy and my parents bought me a suit. Do you really want to wear that?"

"I don't have anything else! If you don't like it...."
She turned away from him, flushing.

"Hey. Calm down. You even sound like I did. I was afraid my friends would see me in a tie and laugh at me. You look fine. Very professional. It just isn't what I think of when I think of you."

"What do you think of?" she challenged. "Am I some waif you need to put decent clothes on?"

"I think of a beautiful young woman who would knock everyone's eyes out if she didn't go around with grass stains on her knees." Before Chela knew he was going to do it, Magadan had taken her arms in his large hands and was pulling her close for a kiss on the forehead. "Don't worry. You look fine. I like everything you wear." He glanced down at her with a mischievous glint in his eyes. "Most of all I like you with nothing on."

Chela buried her head in Magadan's chest, not asking herself why she was so quick to assume this trusting stance. She loved feeling his arms around her arms, his lips on her hair. Women did lean on men, and men leaned on women. It wasn't such a hard lesson to learn after all. "I haven't heard from Kohl," she said after a silence that spread over several minutes.

Gently Magadan pushed her away, although he still held on to her. "I don't want to talk about him."

Neither do I, Chela admitted to herself as they were closing the door to her house behind them. Kohl, the catalyst that had brought them together, was unimportant.

She'd never thought of clothes shopping as an adventure. But with Magadan with her, Chela was looking forward to the next hour. She'd think about whether it was right or wrong later.

Obviously Magadan had given serious thought to what they were doing. He drove to an expensive dress shop in a small mall at the base of the east hills. Chela hesitated momentarily, uneasy as always about going to that part of town. But she'd come this far, she couldn't back down now. When they were inside and waiting for the saleslady to join them, Magadan admitted that he had little experience with such things. "I feel like a bull in a china shop. I don't know what I'm looking for. I just know I'll know when I find it."

Chela was too busy looking around to pay much attention to what Magadan was telling her. Unlike the department stores she went to when she absolutely had to have something to wear, there were few dresses on the racks. But something about their placement and the tastefully made-up mannequins told her Magadan was thinking in terms of more money than she'd ever spent on herself before. Next to the counter with the cash register were a few displays of jewelry, fragile gold necklaces, large dinner rings, bejeweled dinner bags. Chela gulped nervously. What was she doing here?

She didn't have long to ponder the question. Maga-

dan took over with the air of someone who'd handled
all kinds of situations in his life and was equal to this
one as well. He told the petite, middle-aged saleslady
wearing a tailored dress that he was looking for something that could be dressed up for evening wear and yet
versatile enough for less elegant occasions. "Something that highlights her coloring and lets her wear her
hair the way it is," he said as if Chela was a mannequin
herself.

If the saleslady saw anything unusual about either
Chela or Magadan, she kept her thoughts to herself.
"With that coloring you can wear anything," she said,
smiling expansively at Chela. "In fact, I know just the
dress." Before Chela could open her mouth, the clerk
was steering her into a dressing room. Chela had barely
removed her blazer when the clerk returned with a
cloud of peach fabric draped over her arm.

The dress, Chela admitted even before she was in it,
was the most exquisite thing she'd ever seen or felt.
The fabric, according to the clerk, was a crepe, which
gave it its soft drape. There was the barest hint of
sleeve, which left most of Chela's long, slim, dark arms
exposed. There was no collar; instead the delicately
shaded bodice fabric crossed in front and was caught in
a gathered waistline concealed by a sash belt. The
crossed fabric dipped low enough to expose just a hint
of breast, a fact that both embarrassed and intrigued
Chela. The gathered skirt was the palest peach near the
waistline but steadily darkened until it reached a vibrant hue at the hem, falling above knee length in front
but dipping to midcalf on the sides.

"Perfect," the clerk breathed. "I've had a lot of

women try this dress on, but most of them look washed out in it."

Chela was concerned about only one thing. "How much is it?"

"Don't ask," the clerk laughed.

If Magadan was taken aback by the dress's price tag, he didn't show it. In fact when Chela emerged from the dressing room, he didn't say anything for more than a minute. As she nervously modeled the garment, he stared at her without blinking, his eyes darker than she remembered. Finally he said something about her needing shoes to go with the dress and then rose to accompany the clerk to the cash register. Confused, Chela hurried back into the dressing room and quickly changed back into her blazer and skirt. Why had she agreed to this insanity? she wondered. Magadan had shown more enthusiasm over ice cream. It was all wrong. He shouldn't be buying her clothes. But when she came out, Magadan was looking at a slim gold chain. Wordlessly he held it up to her throat and then nodded.

They were back in the car and heading toward the shoe store the clerk suggested before Magadan spoke. "You didn't even try on anything else."

"Did you want me to? Magadan, how much did it cost?"

"That's my secret. It would have been worth it no matter what it cost. Do you have any idea what you look like in it?" His voice held a note of awe.

"No. You didn't say whether you liked it or not. If you're regretting—"

For answer Magadan pulled over to the side of the

road, took her in his arms, and kissed her with an intensity that spread quickly through her body. "I've never seen anything so beautiful," he whispered as he was reentering the stream of traffic.

Chela glanced at him and then, not trusting her emotions, concentrated on the road. Beautiful? Was she really beautiful? The way Magadan said it, she believed him.

It took Magadan twice as long to settle on a pair of shoes as it had to purchase the dress, but Chela, who had always thought of clothes buying as a necessary chore, didn't grow impatient. She still couldn't quite believe that this money was being spent on her by a man who kept a part of himself separate from her, as she did in turn. She wondered how they could be deriving such obvious pleasure from what they were doing this evening when they still circled around each other like wary strangers in much of their relationship.

At last Magadan gave the nod to a pair of high-heeled shoes that Chela wasn't sure would hold together because the straps were so thin. He sighed deeply as he was putting his change back in his wallet. "I think I need a beer. This has been an exhausting expedition."

Five minutes later they were in a dimly lit but elegantly decorated bar where business people came to unwind or share a quiet meal. Chela let Magadan steer her into a booth and even let him order a glass of wine for her. "It isn't lobster, but why don't we have dinner here," Magadan suggested. "Unless you want to invite me over to your place to eat."

Chela thought of tomato soup and cheese sandwiches and gave him a rueful grin. "I don't think what I have to offer can hold a candle to this." She glanced around, her nerve endings recording the dark interior with walls that reminded her of a cave. She should be anxious and uncomfortable, wanting to flee the place for the familiar surroundings of an orchard and fresh air, but the anxiety she expected to flood over her didn't come. As Magadan reached across the small table and took her cool hand, Chela realized that he was responsible for her relaxed, comfortable feeling.

"I didn't think about your not liking closed-in places," he said. "Let me know if it gets to you."

"Thank you," she whispered. No, it wasn't getting to her. But she wasn't sure she wanted to reveal enough of herself to admit that he made the difference. "Have you been here before?" she asked, skirting around her thoughts.

Magadan nodded. "A few times. A lot of business deals are made here. I hope you like the wine."

It was Chela's turn to nod. So he was skirting around certain things, too. It shouldn't bother her. She should be used to that quality in him. "I'm not much of a drinker," she admitted. "I've tried what the migrants drink, but it gives me a headache."

"I wouldn't be surprised. It's probably aged at least a week. This is different."

Magadan was right. The cool liquid slid easily down her throat and settled in her stomach. Chela hadn't finished her first glass before she realized she would have to limit what she drank on an empty stomach.

It wasn't lobster and drawn butter, but the small steaks and salad the Blue Max restaurant served tasted better than anything Chela had eaten in months. When a couple of men came over to talk to Magadan and stole glances in Chela's direction, she dropped her eyes and concentrated on her meal. Did it bother Magadan to be seen with her? She had no skill in small talk and shied away from flirting glances. Despite her skirt and blazer she knew her world was light-years from the one she was in tonight.

"It's a rat race," Magadan said after he'd finished talking to the men about a shipping problem one of them was having with his business. "I don't know why I got myself wrapped up in this. Sometimes I wish I was back in Mexico."

Chela lifted her eyes to meet Magadan's. "You mentioned Mexico before. Was that where you learned to speak Spanish?"

"I learned before I went there. I knew I was going to be hiring Mexican labor and needed to be able to communicate with them." He sighed. "That's history. I'd rather forget that time."

"Why? You didn't like the poverty?"

Magadan acknowledged her challenge. "It isn't all poverty. Chela, I wasn't going to tell you this because I've a pretty good idea what your reaction will be. But I was involved in drilling for oil in Mexico."

"Oil?" Chela frowned and then stiffened as realization sank in. The discovery of oil in Mexico had turned out to be the country's downfall. Too much money too fast had hit the country, overheating a shaky economy until inflation became a runaway plague. Yes, much of the blame had to be absorbed by the Mexican government for borrowing capital at high interest rates. But when the oil companies discovered that the bottom was dropping out of the oil market and shut down, they left a staggering unemployment rate behind. "You owned an oil company?"

Magadan nodded, reluctantly, it seemed to her. "Not by myself. I didn't have the capital for that. But I was the head of a group of businessmen who invested in a company. I was the one who moved to Mexico to oversee its operation."

"And you pulled out when the bottom dropped out of the market?" Chela stopped eating.

"That's what a businessman does. He regroups, redefines his options."

"And to hell with those you leave behind?" Chela pushed back her plate and stared across the small expanse at the man. "You landed on your feet, your workers didn't," she accused. "You aren't unemployed."

"No, I'm not. Chela, look, I'm not proud of what happened in Mexico. I didn't know what would happen to the economy there."

"Didn't you!" With effort Chela kept her voice low enough so those around them couldn't hear. "You said you're a businessman. I can't believe you didn't know what the risks might be."

"I do now. Hindsight is a wonderful thing."

"Isn't it!" she spat at him. "It's just a shame you didn't have the foresight to provide some job security for your employees." Chela didn't want to say anything more. There were thoughts, emotions, pounding in her brain, but they didn't need to be said. All she wanted was to be alone, to think, to get away from Joe Magadan.

He didn't stop her. As Chela pushed herself to her

feet and made her way quickly through the narrow aisles, she could feel his eyes boring into her back, but Magadan didn't come after her.

Good! She didn't want him to! Chela wanted to walk alone through the now-quiet streets. She didn't care that her house was five miles away and she would have to walk in shoes she wasn't accustomed to. It would take at least five miles for her to sort out the few sentences Magadan had spoken.

So his and other companies had gone into Mexico with promises of employment and easy money for hundreds of workers. For a while the country had reaped the benefits of the unaccustomed boost to its economy, the money the government was spending on capital improvements. Everyone was raking in the money—for a little while. And then the bottom dropped out of the oil market and the Mexican people were left to pick up the pieces.

Magadan had regrouped, redefined his options. He wasn't suffering from the consequences.

How could she think the man a humanitarian? Chela asked herself. What a joke that was! Let him have his secrets. Let Magadan figure out what he was going to do with Kohl after she told him she didn't want anything to do with him.

Kohl! No. As an image of Kohl entered her mind, Chela realized she couldn't back out of the commitment to trap him now. Kohl was the chain that would continue to link her to Magadan.

Men like Kohl couldn't be allowed to continue their evil ways. It would take people like Chela and Magadan to stop them.

A part of Chela expected Magadan to come after her, but as the miles slowly slid under her feet, she gave up listening for the sound of his truck. By the time she reached the country road her house was on, she was willing to admit that she had needed this time alone but for reasons much more complex than cooling down. There were so many things about Magadan that needed to be sorted out, so many emotions that had to be brought out into the open one by one and examined.

What she'd learned by the time she started on the last mile was that walking out on Magadan was a futile gesture. No matter what she thought of his actions while in Mexico, she couldn't get the man out of her mind or her heart. Hadn't he warned her that she wasn't going to like what he had to say? He at least had been honest, although she realized now that it had cost him to admit his part in the downward spiral of Mexico's economy.

Chela wasn't perfect, so what gave her the right to cast stones at others? Her denial of his humanitarian qualities was done during those first moments of anger. After all, she did have proof that he was concerned with people, with improving the lot of the Mexicans living in the United States. He'd brought treats for a soccer team and was spearheading an attempt to put Kohl out of operation. Whether he was trying to atone for what had happened in Mexico or whether he'd been born with the desire to reach beyond himself wasn't the issue.

If only there weren't those dark, hidden parts of his life!

Was she getting in too deep with Magadan? For the

first time in her life, Chela was letting someone beyond her defenses. It was almost as if she could smell the danger. Exposed emotions meant risking pain. She'd never taken that risk before; she wouldn't start now. Walking home alone, letting herself into her house, and dropping her blazer and skirt on the bed without anyone to see, was better, safer than having Magadan here. When and if he made contact with her again, she would have placed a barrier around her emotions. They would be partners, nothing more.

And if her heart quailed at the decision she'd made? Chela's heart had been wounded before—at her mother's death, her father's deception. She would survive.

If it hadn't been for the sheriff's unexpected appearance at the Blue Max, Magadan would have been in his truck looking for Chela. As it was, he was now looking at tired gray eyes set in a crinkled face instead of the black eyes framed by ebony hair that he longed to see.

"You've told me everything except what you think of the young lady in question," Kenneth Duff said as he sipped on a beer, his head propped up by his free hand. "I take it she's holding up her end of the bargain. You haven't told her, have you?"

Magadan shook his head. When he first met Chela, he was determined to keep his secret because he was convinced the truth would allow Kohl to slip through his fingers. He was just as determined now, but the reason had ceased to be business and had become personal. His fear now, if that was what the emotion was, was that the truth would end something good. "It's no picnic earning her trust when there's so much I can't tell her," Magadan said, hoping his voice gave away nothing of his personal involvement.

"I don't doubt that for a moment," Kenneth laughed. "That's one woman I wouldn't want to tangle with. She looks like someone who needs a blanket wrapped around her, but she has claws and she knows how to use them. I take it you haven't been able to tame her."

"Far from it," Magadan admitted. "Her claws are just as sharp as they ever were, not that I can blame her. It comes with surviving in a world she didn't plan. In fact, she gave me a lesson just before you showed up."

Kenneth shook his head but didn't disagree with Magadan. Instead he sighed. "There's something you better know. A certain someone is back in town."

Magadan sucked in a ragged breath. Hadn't tonight been hard enough with Chela walking out on him? "You're sure?"

"Damn sure. One of my deputies saw him coming out of a bar the other day. I thought after what happened, well, the man's damn lucky he isn't in prison. I don't know of anyone who'd give him a job. Why he wants to come back here is beyond me, considering everything that's happened to him. Something tells me he's hooking up with Kohl again."

Magadan had to agree. "Don't you know anything more about what he's up to?"

"Not yet I don't." Again Kenneth sighed. "I wish I could tell you I was going to put one of my men on him, tail him until we were sure he was keeping his nose clean. But the truth of the matter is I don't have the manpower. The budget doesn't stretch that far."

"Maybe he's going to turn into an honest man." There was bitter irony in Magadan's statement. "You'd think he'd learn something from having all the props knocked out from under him."

"Yeah, and maybe I'm going to discover a long-lost rich uncle. Once a snake, always a snake." The sheriff took another swallow. "I thought you should know considering what you did. I don't think he's capable of violence, but you never know."

"Look," Magadan said after a long silence. "You let me know if you find out anything else about our mutual friend. I don't think he's going to be looking me up." He thought, momentarily, of the house in the hills but dismissed the possibility that the man would come there. "I don't like not knowing why he's back here. I never figured him to return."

"I didn't either. But there's no law stopping him. The slate's wiped clean as far as the courts and banks are concerned. He hasn't done anything—yet."

Was that true? Magadan wondered after he'd left the Blue Max and was getting into his truck. If Kohl and his former partner were working together again....

Damn! There wasn't a thing he could do about that. He'd have to keep things going the way they were with Chela, try to patch up their disagreement, and turn things back to where the focus was on Kohl, not something that had happened in Mexico years ago. He wasn't going to say anything about his concern that Kohl might not be working alone after all until he had some proof. That was his worry, not Chela's. He'd continue to see her, if she'd let him. Surely she wouldn't back out of their arrangement because of something that belonged in the past.

And if they were able to find their way back to the relationship that existed before an hour ago.... Magadan's body responded to that possibility. When he first spotted her in the orchard, he had thought Chela the most beautiful woman he'd ever seen. That impression hadn't changed. But now it was more. His response was no longer simply physical. Now his heart was involved.

Magadan was on the road Chela lived on almost before he was aware of it. Caution told him he should wait until she had had a chance to calm down, but he'd let her walk five miles. He had to make sure she'd gotten home safely. Would she open the door to him?

Chela was curled up in her rocking chair, staring without seeing at the TV screen, the evening's paper folded on her lap. For the first time since she'd moved into it, her house felt empty and she was almost glad to hear the knock on the door.

Chela was on her feet when the thought hit her. Was Kohl outside? She pulled her robe tighter around her and reknotted the belt around her slender waist. She could hurry into her bedroom and throw on some clothes, but she didn't.

The shadowy figure waiting on the dark porch was one she wanted to see—despite herself.

"Can I come in?" Magadan asked.

Chapter Seven

"Is there something you want?" Chela asked. Although her heart was pounding in her throat, she managed to keep her voice emotionless.

"You know there is." Magadan's voice was sharp, his words clipped. "I wanted to make sure you got home okay. May I come in?"

Chela stepped back, accepting the change in the room as he entered it, and closed the door behind him. How was she going to get him to leave now that he was inside? She retreated and found her way to the rocker. She picked up the newspaper as if to read it. "I'm home."

"I can see that. I would have come after you but—"

"It's just as well," Chela interrupted. "I had a lot of thinking to do. About what you told me."

"Did you come to any conclusions?"

Chela gave up the pretense of looking at the newspaper and fastened her eyes on his. "In a way. I appreciate your honesty. You didn't have to tell me any of that." Her smile was bitter. "After all, you won't tell me anything about your present life. I should be grateful that you said anything about your past."

Magadan held up his hand, effectively stopping her. "You didn't stay around long enough to hear the rest of what I wanted to tell you. I did more than just regroup when I left Mexico."

"Oh."

"How do you think I got to know Ortez?"

"Ortez? What does he have to do with this?" she asked.

"Plenty. Ortez was my foreman. He's running his own business now because of the skills he learned while working for me. Ortez's younger brother is going to college on a scholarship I provided. That's what I did before I left Mexico." Magadan sat down on the couch opposite Chela, but his eyes never left hers. "I went to the university and set up a scholarship program in my name. I provide for two new students a year to go to college."

"Oh." It was the second time in the space of a minute that Chela had said the word, but she couldn't think of anything else.

"That's right," Magadan pressed. "Okay, so my company wasn't the best thing to ever hit Mexico, but it wasn't all bad. Remember, I didn't know the bottom was going to drop out any more than anyone else did. I lost all the capital I'd put into the project. At least a few people are getting the chance to improve themselves. Ortez's brother had been working on his family's farm before he got the scholarship. When he's done, the farm is going to be able to compete in today's market."

"Ortez's family must be grateful to you."

"I don't want anyone's gratitude," Magadan said sharply. "I don't believe in putting anyone in my debt.

What do you want me to do, solve the country's unemployment problem single-handedly?"

"Of course not." Chela's intensity matched Magadan's. "I—I'm pleased to hear what you're doing."

"Are you? I wasn't sure you would be."

Why shouldn't I, Magadan? Chela asked silently. *I feel it in you, your intensity, your determination. You're the kind of man who would make amends for a mistake.* "I shouldn't be surprised that you'd drive out here to find out whether I'd gotten home, should I?" she said. "After all, it's in keeping with your character."

"That's me, the boy scout. I'm sorry. I meant to follow you, but I met someone before I could leave. There were things we had to discuss."

"Things you aren't going to tell me about, that's what you're saying isn't it, Magadan?" she asked bitterly.

Magadan groaned. "It can't be helped, Chela. You have to trust me."

"Of course, I do." Chela tucked her bare feet up under her robe and wrapped her hands around her knees. Her insteps ached from walking on heels, but the pulsing headache between her eyes was worse. "You know I do." She started to massage her instep.

Magadan's eyes made their way down her body and fastened on her fingers. "Do you have blisters? I'm sorry."

"No," she admitted. "But my feet ache. I'm not used to heels."

"I think I like you better in tennis shoes. At least that's what I'm used to seeing you in."

"And old denims?"

Magadan grinned. "It's not the packaging that counts. It's the woman underneath."

Chela didn't blush. Maybe it was the night and her exhausted state. Maybe it was the pleasant time they'd had together before he'd told her about his oil connections. At any rate she didn't think before saying what was on her mind. "Do you know what I said the first day I saw you? One of the workers said maybe you were looking for a woman. I told him you'd have to have me dead. I don't feel like that anymore."

Magadan leaned forward. "Why?"

"I don't know. Maybe because I now know that you hadn't come to the orchard looking for a woman."

"Can you be sure?" Magadan's eyes were burning with a challenge she could weather only by locking her eyes with his. "Maybe this is what all this is about. Maybe I've wanted you from that first day."

"Did you?"

"I think you know the answer to that."

Chela didn't speak. The truth was, the few words they'd just spoken had stripped away the layers and exposed what their eyes were already saying. Arguments, walking five miles, secrets, had nothing to do with what was happening between them. The only thing that mattered was her resolve to build a barrier around her heart was crumbling. She didn't move when Magadan got to his feet and came to stand over her; she didn't speak when he reached out and pulled her to him.

Chela lifted her head, a wild animal seeking something it didn't have a name for but needed in order to go on living. Magadan's gentle lips on hers was the start. She'd been given the first morsel necessary for survival.

"You don't hate me?" he asked.

"I tried. I don't think I could ever hate you, Magadan," she answered before he stopped her with his lips. He had looked almost afraid to come inside. She should be thinking about why that was, but she couldn't. There was only one thing she could think about.

Magadan's hand was reaching past the barriers of her robe, pulling the belt free and helping the fabric slide off her breasts. As the evening air touched her breasts, Chela sensed them responding. She trembled slightly, knowing how untested she was in such matters. Was she supposed to pull back, not expose her body this freely?

It was too late for such questions. Magadan had her robe all the way open so that the fabric barely clung to her shoulders and upper arms. From throat to feet, she was naked. As she stood helpless before him, she trembled anew. His hands began a slow exploration that began at her throat.

Magadan's fingers were on the side of her neck, her collarbone, the swell of her breasts. Slowly, so slowly that she thought she would scream with wanting it, he finally took possession of her breasts. They surged to life within the warm human prison, and Chela swayed slightly, forgetting that muscles were needed to keep her from collapsing. She wanted him to keep his hands where they were for the rest of the night, but when she thought she would sob from the emotions he was unleashing, his fingers dipped lower, tracing slowly the outline of her ribs.

"God! I've wanted to do this for so long. Don't tell me to stop," Magadan groaned.

Putting an end to this exquisite torture was the last thing Chela wanted. Before tonight she had thought of her body as a tool necessary to propel her through life. Now she was learning that it was capable of receiving and recording an emotion that went to the center of her being.

Magadan's hands returned to her shoulders and slowly, reverently, it seemed to her, pushed back the robe until it slid down her limp arms and landed in a heap at her feet. His eyes were hooded, giving her no access to his thoughts.

"I said we'd make love when you were ready for it," Magadan said in the same ragged tone he'd used a minute before. "I have to know how you feel."

Chela felt everything and nothing, emotions, sensations of a type that couldn't be translated into words. Yes, she wanted him. She wanted to feel his flesh against hers, to lie beside him in bed and give her body to him. But she feared that would be too much of a surrender.

"I don't know" was all she could tell him.

Magadan groaned but didn't leave her. Instead he took her hands and placed them on his chest where it showed through the open buttons of his shirt. He taught her to take his chest hairs between her fingers and run her fingertips over the ridge of his collarbone. Chela's fingertips came alive against his flesh, but it was deeper, lower in her body that the greatest response was taking place. The uncivilized little girl who'd been taken from a migrant camp was once more alive.

Chela didn't ask permission before she grabbed the

hem of his shirt and pulled it over his head. If he could strip her naked, she had the right to do this. The truth was, she couldn't stop herself.

She wasn't sure which of them was the first to take the step that pressed their naked flesh together. She stretched her neck upward until she could reach Magadan's mouth. Her lips parted slightly, giving him access to the sensual cage beyond her teeth. Their kiss was another step toward surrender, another step that maybe couldn't be taken back.

"Do you have any idea what you're doing to me?" Magadan groaned. "I promised you this wouldn't happen until you wanted it. But I don't know if I can stop."

"I won't ask you that," she started shyly, and then suddenly turned bold. "Don't stop. Magadan, I want you."

A shuddering sigh racked Magadan's body. He lifted Chela in his arms and held her close to his body. She wrapped her arms around his neck and buried her head in his chest. Her hair tumbled forward covering both of them. Magadan stumbled slightly as they went through the entrance to her bedroom, but she felt safer than she ever had in her life. As he lowered her onto the bed, Chela felt the rough finish of her handmade Mexican coverlet against her backbone, the fabric scratching her hips.

Chela didn't take her eyes off Magadan as he removed the rest of his clothes. She thought about getting up and pulling back the earth-toned coverlet so they could make love on sheets, but the feel of familiar fabric on her flesh was adding to her already increased sensitivity. Magadan would have to accept that symbol of her world.

A moment later Chela wasn't thinking about the rough fabric or the night air. Her thoughts went no further than Magadan's lips on hers, his hands exploring every inch of fiery flesh.

"I knew this was going to happen sometime," Magadan whispered as they clung together, readying themselves for fulfillment.

"You were that sure?"

"It's what I've wanted since the day I saw you. I didn't believe there was anything strong enough to stop it from happening."

The something Magadan was talking about had to do with mutual secrets, but Chela wasn't going to think about that now. She was going to arch her spine, cling to Magadan's shoulders with iron fingers, and try to remember to breathe while he brought her body to a point it had never been before. The spot that existed deep inside Chela quickly absorbed the heat in her flesh. Flames consumed her mind, her heart, her very soul. She didn't exist beyond the act of lovemaking. She didn't want to.

When it was over, when they had both been satisfied, Chela tried to come to grips with how much time had passed, but it didn't matter. They'd made love. Magadan's body was next to hers on the boldly colored blanket. He had taken her on a journey she didn't know existed. Whatever differences remained between them had been erased—for the moment.

"Do you want me to leave?" Magadan asked after a long time.

Chela stirred and pulled her mind back from the unthinking place it had been. Her answer came in the form of an arm around his shoulder and a slim, tanned leg draped over his.

In the morning they made love again, and then Magadan soaped her back after she'd climbed into her bathtub. "You do that very well, Magadan," Chela sighed. She arched her spine, acknowledging the heady, sensual feeling.

He gently directed her head until she had no choice but to face his eyes. "When are you going to call me Joe?"

Chela realized she had come a long way last night in giving herself to Magadan, but she was unsure that now was the time when she would feel safe calling him by his first name. The fear of total openness held her back. "Don't rush it, Magadan," she warned, her eyes as unrelenting as his. "It may never happen. I can't guarantee—"

Magadan kissed her wet face in interruption and then turned away. "I wouldn't be here if I believed that, Chela."

After he'd left her, Chela continued to stare at the door. She was wet from her bath, but there was another source for the moisture on her face. Chela was crying silent, wondering tears. This feeling that she wanted to share herself with someone else was too new for her to understand it fully, but not so foreign that she wasn't aware of the loneliness that had existed before Magadan had come into her life. How she was going to resolve that feeling could require more of her than she ever thought possible.

She'd dried her hair and wrapped a large towel around her before leaving the bath. She could hear Magadan rummaging around the kitchen, grumbling to himself as he opened and closed cupboards. "Don't you have any coffee around here?" he mumbled. "Don't tell me you're one of those health-food fanatics who thinks coffee is bad for them."

"I thought you were in a good mood in the morning," Chela quipped, relieved to throw off heavy thoughts. "No, I don't have coffee, but it's because it gives me the shakes, nothing more."

Magadan frowned and then smiled as he saw what she was wearing. "I'll have to remember to bring some over."

"Does that mean you'll be coming back?"

"You better believe it, lady. You're not going to get rid of me that easy."

Chela didn't want to get rid of him, but she didn't know how to respond, either. "Are you going to be late for work?" she asked instead. Then she realized her question wasn't as innocent as it sounded. Perhaps he would drop some clue about himself.

"I'm my own boss," he answered. "No one can bawl me out if I'm late. But you're right." He sighed loudly. "Much as I'd like to hang around here and see what you're going to replace that towel with, I've got to leave."

"Oh?"

"I'm expecting some deliveries. Besides, I have to stop somewhere for a cup of coffee."

"When will I see you again?" she asked, suddenly feeling like a shy schoolgirl.

Instead of answering, Magadan grabbed the top of her towel and pulled her close to him. He kissed her long and deep before speaking. "Tonight."

Chela could only nod. She was too shaken by his kiss to trust herself to speak. She didn't try to stop him when he walked out the front door. She'd turned around and was heading toward her bedroom when he came back in again. "I almost forgot something," he said, handing her the box with her peach dress in it. "Take good care of it. I want to see you in it as soon as possible."

"Maybe I'll wear it to work today," she teased.

"You do and I'll have to ravage you in the middle of the orchard." He kissed her again, briefly. "Tonight."

Tonight, Chela thought as she dressed in her usual outfit and climbed into her Jeep. Tonight, she thought while she was sitting in the middle of an orchard with three Mexicans leaning over the book opened on her lap. Tonight, she reminded herself after she'd convinced a teenage girl with a baby in her arms to start attending English night classes.

Chela was sweaty and tired when she stopped by the grocery store for coffee and some groceries. The air-conditioned store made her shiver, so getting back into her Jeep was a relief. She was aware that a couple of middle-aged women were staring at her, but she'd seen looks like that before and was able to dismiss them. They lived in different worlds, she thought. Chela didn't understand theirs; they didn't understand hers.

As she turned onto her road, Chela remembered how she'd gotten home last night. Stalking away from Magadan while he stared after her had been a reckless move, one she didn't fully comprehend. She wasn't one to turn away from a confrontation. Besides, a man capable of putting her at ease in the dark confines of the Blue Max deserved better than to be left to stare at an uneaten meal. As she slowed for her driveway, Chela toyed with the idea of preparing a special meal for Magadan. It was the kind of thing other women did for the men in their lives.

There was a car in her carport, but it wasn't until Chela was turning off the road that she acknowledged its presence. In the same instant she recognized it as the glittering one Kohl drove.

Chela picked up her bag of groceries and got out of the Jeep, breathing deeply. Her tennis shoes made a dry, slapping sound as she climbed the three steps to her front door. She reached for the knob without pulling out her key. The door was unlocked.

"You're a trusting one," she heard Kohl challenge even before she was all the way in the room.

"I knew it would be you." Chela walked past the figure on the couch, dropped her groceries on the kitchen table, and slowly returned to the living room. She hadn't had enough time to get back into the role of a lovesick woman, frantic to have her lover brought to her. Would Kohl notice? "You're back. Did you get in touch with Ortez?"

"Sit down," he ordered. "Do you have anything to drink here?"

"No." Chela sat down as he ordered and folded her fingers together in what she hoped was a gesture of anxiety. "Did you see him?"

"He didn't tell you? Lovers talk to each other over the phone when they can't be in bed together."

"He's hard to reach. I tried twice this week," Chela

said quickly, praying she was saying the right things. "He's looking for work. I don't always know where he'll be."

Kohl smiled the lipless smile that turned Chela's stomach. "You're a lush woman, Chela. What do you want with a skinny man?"

Chela paused, wondering if Kohl was trying to trick her. Magadan's description of Ortez was of a man who loved the outdoor life but was committed to expanding his mind even if that meant sitting at a desk for long hours. Chela knew that Ortez worked at keeping his body in shape. "If you think he's skinny, then you don't see him the way I do," she said warily.

"Maybe. And maybe I can't believe anything you tell me." Kohl cracked his knuckles loudly. "You wouldn't do that to me, would you, Chela? You wouldn't be that stupid."

"We've been over that before." The man expected her to expose her hate for him. That required no acting. "You wouldn't be here if you thought I was lying."

"Maybe. And maybe I'm here for another reason."

"I don't want to play games, Kohl," Chela said, forcing the anger to retreat in her voice. "You saw Ortez. What happens now? Are you going to bring him to me? His problems with the government—"

"Not so fast. A businessman doesn't succeed if he rushes into situations without sniffing things out thoroughly first. One wrong step and it's all over. You should know that, Chela. You know what brings a man to his knees."

Chela didn't want to talk about that. She was supposed to be a lovesick woman. "Are you going to bring Ortez to me?" she repeated.

"Maybe. And maybe not. What's it worth to you, Chela?"

"You know what I can pay." Was he trying to trip her up? Chela thought she knew all the twists and turns of Kohl's mind, but she couldn't be sure. He was right about one thing. He wouldn't still be free, running his despicable business if he hadn't learned to keep one jump ahead. "I can't afford any more."

"Don't be so sure about that." Kohl laughed. "Everything can be negotiated. I've already made one trip to make sure you're telling me the truth. That increases my expenses."

So that was what he was getting at. His greed knew no bounds. He was going to feel her out, see if she would up the ante. Slowly, testing the direction the conversation was taking, Chela started. "That isn't my fault. I didn't ask you to go down there. I just want Ortez with me."

"And you thought I would take what you say at face value. I'm afraid not, my wild one. Don't take me for a fool. You and I have growled at each other too long for me to trust anything you say. You should know that. You want your precious Ortez with you, you pay for it."

"I can't," Chela said with what she hoped was the right amount of hopelessness in her voice.

"I think you can. Another thousand isn't going to kill you, Chela. Love has no limits, not even financial."

"One thousand dollars...." Chela pretended to be weighing what Kohl had told her. She could sense his relentless eyes on her and was grateful that she wore more than a bathrobe today. "That much more?"

"That's the way it is. There is another alternative involving your body, but I don't like having to keep one eye open for a knife in my back." Kohl sounded as if they were settling on the price of a dozen eggs. "I have expenses. Overhead. You want to be reunited with your lover, you come up with the money."

"I don't have it, not now."

"Get it, or we'll never discuss this matter again."

"You'll have to give me a little time." God, she hated the begging tone she deliberately let enter her voice. "I don't know where I'll get the money. Can't you...."

Kohl smiled and rose to his feet. "I'll be back in two days, Chela. I want you to have all of it here waiting for me."

She shook her head. Now she could stop playing this hated role and go back to being herself. "No," she said firmly. "Half now, half when Ortez is here."

Kohl's "no" was so sharp that it was almost a physical slap. "I want all of it now or it's no deal."

Chela, too, rose to her feet. "Half now, half when I see Ortez. Otherwise you get nothing. It's the only way I can ensure Ortez's safety."

She was ready for Kohl's menacing step, and yet there was no way she could stop herself from leaning away from him. The man's breath assaulted her nostrils, but her retreat was caused by more than that—she knew what he was capable of. "All. Now. You'll have to trust me to deliver Ortez."

Chela laughed, relieved that her voice betrayed none

of her tension. "I don't trust you any farther than I can throw you, Kohl. I know what you've done in the past. That's why it has to be the way I say."

He frowned. For a moment she thought he was going to strike her. Instead he brought himself a step closer to her rigid body and swayed over her. "You drive a hard bargain, my wild one. I think you're going to regret it."

"I regret everything that brings us together," Chela said, knowing she was playing with the slimy man's self-control but also knowing he expected her to display her hatred of him. "But you can't threaten me."

"You don't think so? You're a fool then, Chela, a fool. I'll give you two days, and when I return you'll understand why you can't double-cross me."

He wasn't bluffing. That was what made Kohl such a formidable opponent—the man never made threats he couldn't back up. "I'll have half of the money ready for you in two days," she said, clamping a lid on the emotions that threatened to ruin everything she'd worked to achieve.

"And I'll have a surprise for you." Another cold smile contorted Kohl's face. "One that will bring you in line." He took another step and came so close that Chela was forced to move away to keep him from touching her.

He took another step, a cat relishing the stalking of a mouse. Chela raged against the game but knew no way to end it. If she stood her ground, he would touch her and that she couldn't bear. Backing away from him was her only option. She didn't stop until he had her pressed against the wall of her living room. *I hate you,*

Kohl. I hate you with every fiber in me, was what she was thinking. Instead she willed her voice to remain steady. "What kind of surprise?"

He laughed, revealing teeth that seldom if ever felt a toothbrush. "Wouldn't you like to know? But that would ruin things, wouldn't it? I want you to be aware of how far my influence reaches, to remember that there's no way you can get away from me." As if to emphasize his point, he placed his hands on either side of Chela and rested his palms against the wall. "Ah, my wild one, do you know what I see when I look at you? A prize. The chase would be such a challenge because the prize is worth the effort. You hate me, which makes it all the more intriguing. Do you have any idea what we could accomplish if we worked together? The Mexicans trust you. There would be no end to what we could do together."

"Never!" Chela didn't have to worry about letting her fury show. It was exactly what her adversary expected. "I'd never turn against my people!" She turned her head to the side so she didn't have to feel his hot breath on her lips.

"Your people? Are you forgetting your father's blood running through your veins? Don't be so quick to deny that." His mouth followed hers until they were only inches away. "There are ways of making you faithful to that part of your bloodline."

Suddenly, surely, like a deadly premonition of one's death, Chela saw what Kohl was driving at. "Where is he?" she whispered, wondering at her ability to speak.

"That, Chela Reola, is for me to know and for you to

think about in the black of night. Don't you want to see him? What kind of woman are you not to want to see your own loving father?"

She could tear Kohl's eyes out, bury her nails in his face, but what would she have accomplished other than putting an end to his cruel taunts? "He doesn't want to see me any more than I want to see him," she said, mastering her emotions with an effort. "You're trying to bring back the past. It won't work."

"Don't be so sure." Before Chela could stop him, Kohl had captured her mouth and was branding her with his thin, hard lips. The kiss, if it could be called that, was to establish the relationship between them, to let Chela know that he would never stand for a woman, especially her, to best him at anything.

Finally, when she thought she would lose her mind from the effort of enduring his repulsive touch, Kohl laughed and released her. "Think about it, Chela. Two days, then we'll talk again."

Chela didn't move as he backed away from her, smiling all the time, and made his way to the door. Her last view of him was his smiling yellow teeth and tight lips as he closed the door between them.

For a moment Chela thought she was going to be able to endure it. He was gone. She could hear his car pulling out of the driveway. He would be back in two days to make the contact that would, hopefully, put him out of business. That was what counted, nothing else.

"Damn!" The oath burst from her with a life of its own. She slammed her strong hand against the wall, her fist so tight that her nails dug into the palm of her hand. "Damn you, Kohl! If you—"

The phone rang. At first Chela wasn't going to answer it because she didn't trust herself not to rip the phone out of the wall. But it would be Magadan. He'd come here if she didn't pick up the receiver. She wasn't sure her greeting was loud enough for him to hear.

He said something about coming over shortly, but when she didn't respond beyond a monosyllable, he pressed her for an explanation of her mood.

"Kohl was here when I got home."

"He's gone?"

"Yes." Unexpectedly Chela's anger and agitation escaped. "He doesn't believe in small talk. He left as soon as we'd conducted our business."

"What happened?" Magadan pressed. "Are you going to tell me what he said?"

"Not over the phone," Chela answered shortly. She needed time to pull herself together to drape a solid veil over the past Kohl dredged up.

"I'll be right over," Magadan said and hung up.

Chela replaced the receiver and paced to the window to look out. No, she saw with relief, Kohl hadn't come back. She didn't want Magadan to hurry. In fact she would have preferred he didn't come to see her at all tonight. This wasn't the way a woman was supposed to feel about seeing her lover, was it? But Chela wasn't like most women. She couldn't curl up with her man and whisper sweet nothings until they were ready to make love. Chela had secrets, dark passages in her past. Kohl had trod those passages, and she wasn't sure she could keep that from Magadan.

But, somehow, she had to. Magadan had become special when she didn't know that would happen. Because of him she had to keep that heavy veil over the past.

Chapter Eight

Magadan didn't bother to knock. He barreled through the door like an avenger on his way to do battle. He found Chela in the kitchen measuring granules into a pitcher for iced tea. She turned calmly toward him, her feelings, she thought, well in check. "Don't you believe in knocking?" she asked. "If I'd locked my door, you would have broken it down."

"To hell with the door. What are you doing?"

"Making tea. I'll have us some in a few minutes."

For a moment Magadan seemed fascinated by what she was doing, then suddenly his hand snaked out and stopped her. "That's the fifth tablespoonful you've put in. No one can drink that."

"Oh," Chela said and then watched as Magadan took out about half of the dark grains. When he finally filled the pitcher with water, the resulting liquid was amber, not dirt brown the way it would have been if he'd allowed her to continue. "Do you have to criticize everything I do?" she asked as he was pouring tea over glasses filled with ice.

Magadan gave her an indulgent smile. "I'm just glad

you're not with your migrant kids now. You'd have them so confused they'd wish they were back across the border. He gave you a rough time, didn't he?''

Chela wondered if she'd ever find a way to hide her emotions from Magadan. She was so transparent around him. But suddenly it no longer mattered. She accepted the frosty glass and drank deeply, the cool liquid at least washing away a day spent in the orchards, if not what had happened in her house a few minutes ago. "I hate that man. I could kill him," she said with a conviction that didn't surprise her.

Magadan steered her out of the kitchen and onto the couch in the living room. "I don't think I'd like to have that statement tested if I were Kohl," he said as he joined her. "I just wish I understood why your hatred of him goes so deep."

Never, Magadan. That's something I'll never tell you. "He's going to be back in two days," she said instead. "I told him I'd only give him half of the money now. He wants a thousand more."

"That figures. But I think it's working, Chela." Magadan leaned forward but didn't touch her as if he knew she was on the brink of igniting. "He's falling for it. If he delivers Ortez to you without twisting a few screws, our case won't be as strong. I'm just hoping his greed will make him use Ortez as hostage for more money."

He wouldn't have to use Ortez if he thought he could get to her, Chela acknowledged. If only she could tell Magadan what Kohl was threatening her with, but she'd held that secret all her life. "Can you come up with the money?"

"Of course." Magadan smiled, but the gesture was without warmth. "I figured this would happen. It's part of the game we have to play."

Rage, which Chela thought she'd conquered, surged through her. "It isn't a game, Magadan! Not with me it isn't. You don't know the stakes—" She slammed her glass onto the nearby coffee table and sprang to her feet. She was almost to the door when she realized that this was her home and leaving it made no sense. "Can you have the money in two days?" she asked, her voice revealing none of what her tense, trembling body was saying.

"You let me worry about the money. You have to get control over yourself. That's your job." He joined her by the door but made no comment about her irrational behavior. "Did he hurt you this time?"

Chela stuck out her hands to reveal no marks on her wrists. Magadan didn't have to know of the kiss that had been far greater punishment than any bruise. "Do I look as if I've been hurt?"

"You certainly act like it." Something angry and dangerous flashed in his eyes but died an instant death. "Look, I was going to take you out to dinner tonight. The offer still holds."

She couldn't think of eating, of controlling her emotions enough to enter a restaurant. She shook her head. "You go. I'm not hungry."

Magadan released his breath in an angry hiss. "I'm not going to go eat and leave you here. I'd think you'd have realized that by now. I'll tell you what. You've been out in the sun all day and your hair's clinging to your neck. Go take a bath. It might help you relax."

Yes, that would feel good, Chela admitted. Cold water on her flesh might restore some sense of calm to her nerves. "I don't want you to come into the bathroom," she warned as she turned longing eyes in the direction of the room.

For the first time today he touched her, gentle hands along the side of her neck. "I understand, Chela. I understand you better than you think I do. What I said earlier about our being lovers only when you want it still goes. Now isn't the time, is it?"

She shook her head but didn't move out from under his touch until he steered her into the bathroom and started to fill the tub with water. Maybe he was right about understanding her. She wanted him here—that she wouldn't deny—but now wasn't the time for lovemaking. Kohl's visit and threats had placed her beyond that point. Chela slipped off her shoes but didn't start to undress until Magadan had closed the door behind her.

She washed slowly, thoroughly, erasing from her flesh the imprint made by Kohl's presence. She gave special attention to her mouth, washing and rewashing it until the bitter taste of soap stopped her. Finally she shampooed her hair and rinsed it thoroughly under the tap, taking simple pleasure in the squeaking sounds she could make by running her fingers through the strands. She stepped out, toweled off, and wrapped another towel around her hair.

When she opened the bathroom door, cooking smells reached her, but Chela didn't go to investigate until she'd traded her twin towels for the white sun dress that represented a complete departure from the world that brought her into contact with Kohl.

"I hope you like eggs," Magadan said as she entered the kitchen. "I excel in omelets, but I'm afraid that pushes my culinary talents to their limit." His voice dropped when he turned to face her. "You're beautiful."

Embarrassed, Chela pushed her still-damp hair off her shoulders and wondered, for the first time in her life, what it would do to her features if she was to wear makeup. "I...you've seen this dress before."

"And I hope I never stop seeing you in it. White is your color. That and peach."

Chela dropped her eyes. "You didn't have to fix me anything."

"Yes, I did. I'm starved, and you want to stay home," he reminded her. "It's a good thing you had eggs. There's everything but the kitchen sink in this omelet," he went on conversationally. "Onions, green peppers, chilies. You sure have a lot of vegetables around here."

Chela didn't dare come any closer because she wasn't sure she could keep her hands off his body if she did. Everything had been all wrong before Magadan came into the house. Now it was becoming right again. "Some of the Mexicans have gardens," she explained. "They keep me well supplied."

"I'll have to send them a thank-you card. Sit down. First we eat. Then we'll talk."

Chela wasn't sure she was up to the kind of talking Magadan was hinting at, but by the time she'd finished off the omelet and American fries he'd prepared to go with it, the hollow feeling in her stomach was no longer crawling into her throat. At length she stopped eating and smiled at him across the kitchen table. "I didn't know I was hungry," she admitted. "The Mexican women tell me that a whining baby is a baby with an empty belly."

"You weren't whining," Magadan pointed out. "Something else had you climbing the walls. Now, I want to know all about it."

Chela shook her head and started speaking at the same time. Briefly she explained about Kohl's supposed contact with Ortez and his reasons for increasing the payment. She repeated that he would be back in two days. What she didn't tell him was the part of the conversation that followed.

"Did he threaten you again?"

"When doesn't he threaten? That's the only way he knows how to deal with people," she countered, instead of giving Magadan the answer she knew he wanted.

Magadan frowned. "I want to be here, hidden somewhere when he comes back. When I think of him here with you—"

Chela froze. It would be too dangerous. "No! Kohl would find out. I know the man. We've brought him this far. We can't risk losing him now."

Magadan cocked his head and fixed his eyes on her. "What happened to the confident woman I've always seen before? Something happened to change you. What is it?"

Instead of trying to answer a question she couldn't, Chela turned the conversation around. "Something's changed you, Magadan. You were so willing to have me deal with Kohl before. What's different now?"

Magadan reached across the littered table and took her hand. "I think you know the answer to that. You. You and I have changed. I don't see this the way I used to."

Chela freed her hand and nervously started clearing the table. "You'll have to go back to what you saw before," she tried to point out. "You can't change things this late in the game. Kohl will smell it and slip out of your grip."

"It doesn't matter. Your safety is more important than that." He'd picked up his dishes and was taking them to the sink. "Maybe it was a fool plan from the start, putting you in the position of working with Kohl just because—"

"Just because I'm the only one who would fit in with your plan." Chela turned on him, free at least for the moment of the uncertainties that had assaulted her since her enemy's visit. "You supply the money and the plan, Magadan. I'll do my part."

"I don't like it."

"You don't have to like it." She laughed softly. "You aren't dealing with a helpless female, Magadan. I'm as much of a bulldog as you are. Once I put my teeth into something, I don't give up." *No matter what Kohl sends my way,* she thought.

Magadan put away the salt and pepper without speaking. Then he took her hands and pulled her close to him. "You don't look like any bulldog, Chela. You look like a beautiful, desirable woman, and I feel like protecting you. If you don't like hearing that, I can't help it. That's the way it is."

"You've changed, Magadan," she challenged.

"You've changed me, Chela. If I knew I was going to wind up feeling this way about you...."

She didn't try to draw away. Instead Chela let her body lean toward his, gave acknowledgment to what she'd wanted to do from the moment he walked in the door. She freed her hands and reached up to draw his face down toward hers. "It's just as well you didn't," she said softly, wisely. "Neither of us did."

Those were the last words either of them spoke until they were in the bedroom and Magadan had draped her white dress across the end of the bed. "I don't know what you've done to me," he said, his voice husky. "I've never felt this way toward a woman before. If I didn't know better"—he stopped for a moment to caress her left breast—"I'd think you'd cast a spell over me."

It wasn't a spell, she admitted silently. She didn't know anything about what took place between a man and a woman. "Maybe you should go back to Mexico. The air here might be doing strange things to you."

"The air has nothing to do with this." He kissed a nipple, smiling as a groan escaped her. "Let's see if I can cast any spells of my own and make you forget what happened tonight."

He did. It was still light outside when their bodies joined on the Mexican coverlet. Neither of them was aware of the deepening shadows that swallowed the room and hid the difference between dark and lighter skin.

They dozed briefly, got up, and read the paper together and then, without approval having to be asked or given, made love again and fell asleep with their bodies touching.

Sometime during the night Chela became aware of the breeze coming from her open window brushing across their naked bodies. Instead of getting up to look for her nightshirt, she snuggled closer to Magadan, her arm draped across the broad expanse of his shoulder as he lay on his side. Chela ran her lips lightly over his back before resting her head on her pillow. He had changed everything about the evening, taken her from feeling like she'd been punched in the belly to acknowledging that she'd never felt as secure as she did at this moment.

It was so easy to trust this man. So easy.

Chela continued to feel Magadan's impact on her to cling to while she waited for the next two days to drag by. Although many school officials were still on vacation, she met with the migrant education supervisor to decide what they had to do to make sure each migrant child in the county would be accounted for and given bus route and other essential information. Chela had to cut back on her tutoring in the orchards because she wanted to go to each barrio to make sure parents were aware that their children needed to be registered. Three times she agreed to drive the parents to the various schools to make sure the necessary papers were signed.

The concentration of job activities gave Chela the opportunity to turn her mind away from Kohl and the possibility that he could slip through their net no matter how carefully they'd planned. He had eluded arrest and conviction before. It could happen again. But Chela was immersed in Magadan's warmth and the unreasoning belief that the man could make everything right just by being there.

"You're mighty cheerful," Jeff Cline observed when

Chela volunteered to foot the bill for ice cream for the entire soccer team Thursday afternoon. "You uncover some rich uncle you didn't know existed?"

"Not an uncle," was all Chela would reveal.

"I thought as much." Jeff gave her a playful poke on the arm. "It wouldn't happen to be the guy who showed up here that time, would it? It looked to me as if he wasn't going to go away until you at least gave him the time of day."

Chela laughed. "You're too young to understand such things." She didn't add that she was the one who didn't understand. Yes, Magadan had changed her life. The thing was, she'd never been able to figure out what he'd done to change her.

Friday wasn't the time to think about Magadan and his impact on her life. Friday was for seeing Kohl. When she got off work, Chela toyed with the idea of not going home at all, where she knew Kohl would be sure to try to contact her. But Magadan had come out to the orchard that afternoon with an envelope full of the money she needed. He'd reminded her—as if she needed reminding—that Kohl wasn't a man to be taken lightly. Not going home would only delay the meeting and possibly jeopardize what she'd already worked hard to achieve.

At least Kohl wasn't waiting in her driveway when she turned off the road. Chela hurried inside, fought the urge to lock her door behind her, and called Magadan to let him know that contact hadn't been made yet. "I'm not going to leave here," Magadan said firmly. "And I'm coming over there if I haven't heard from you in a couple of hours."

"I'll be all right," Chela replied. "This meeting isn't

going to be any different from the ones we've had before."

"Maybe, maybe not. I'll be here. Call me."

Where was here? Chela asked as she hung up. Magadan had spent the night at her house, in her bed, with her arms around him, yet she didn't even know where he lived.

She didn't have much time to think about that. The knock on the door came after she'd kicked off her tennis shoes but before she'd had time to pour herself something cool to drink.

Chela walked slowly to the door and opened it with numb fingers. She was ready to face Kohl. But two men stood outside. Even though she knew who else might be there when she opened the door, there was no way she could prepare herself to face Kohl's companion.

"Are you trying to keep us out?" Kohl asked, his words cutting through the whirring sound that had suddenly filled her brain.

A breathy oath escaped from Chela's lips. She clamped down on the sound before it could become more and pulled her eyes toward the coyote. Let the other man come to his own conclusions about her refusal to acknowledge his presence.

Kohl's shirt was sticking to his bony chest and hung limp and damp from his shoulders. Chela focused on that fact, pleased to see that the hot valley afternoon touched weasels as well as people like herself. "You keep your appointments," she said, moving back to let the two men in. She didn't close the door after they were inside; neither did she breathe.

Kohl's companion was the one to close out the sunlight. He was taller than Kohl with too much flesh around his jaws and a belly that hung over his belt. There were still signs that the man had once been athletic, but the years of sitting and letting others do his work had taken their toll. Chela was unprepared for the wave of emotion that assaulted her when she realized he was going bald. It made no sense to feel as if she might scream if she opened her mouth, but she knew the sound was dangerously close to breaking free. Being in the same room with the stranger who was in truth the farthest thing from a stranger was something she'd thought about a hundred times but doubted would ever happen.

So this was her father.

"Aren't you two going to say hello?" Kohl mocked, obviously enjoying the moment. "This should be a touching reunion, father and daughter. What do you think of her, Lou? I thought you said she was a dirty little kid."

"She was the last time I saw her up close."

"I grew up. No thanks to you." Chela deliberately turned her back on the two men and took her usual spot in her recliner. Now that she'd actually faced her father, the worst of the shock was over. He was just a man after all.

"Now, now," Kohl mouthed. "There isn't going to be a fight between you two, is there? This really should be a touching scene. Isn't anyone going to say thanks for my bringing the two of you together?"

"Why did you?" Chela wasn't sure she'd been able to contain her fury, but maybe it didn't matter; he expected her to be emotional. "Lou Dye and I have nothing in common."

"Except that you're blood relatives." Kohl sat down on the couch and with eye contact ordered Lou to take a chair opposite the recliner so that Chela was trapped between the two men.

"That was an accident." Chela pointedly avoided meeting the coyote's eyes; instead, she allowed her eyes the freedom to bore into her father's face, looking for what she didn't know.

"No accident. Your mother and I were married, Chela."

"So she told me. Why?" Chela asked. She hated having to talk to her father, and yet it was a question that had never been answered. "Why did you marry her? You never wanted anything to do with her after I was born."

Lou's voice was almost sad as he answered Chela's question, and he seemed to have difficulty meeting her grinding gaze. "Look at yourself, Chela. Your mother was so much like you at that age. She was a beautiful woman. I wanted her badly."

"You wanted a beautiful woman to show off. That's it, isn't it?" Chela could say those words because she had no feelings for the man who was her father. "And because she wouldn't have you without marriage."

"Her people wouldn't have anything to do with me even after we were married. The marriage was over before you were born. But that isn't why we're here." Lou turned toward Kohl. "Can we get on with this?"

"What's the matter, Lou? Isn't the reunion turning

out the way you wanted it to? Never mind. You can always reconcile with your daughter later.''

"There isn't going to be any reconciliation," Chela spat. "I don't want him here. Why did you bring him?''

"We're getting to that, my wild one." Kohl laughed. "Don't rush things. This has to go my way or not at all. First, the money.''

Chela shook her head. She hadn't had time to switch from confronting her father to talking about the reason for the meeting, but she'd played this scene so many times in her mind that she didn't need time. "First, you tell me when I'll see Ortez.''

Kohl laughed again. "You and I should be working together. We think alike. And we don't move quickly. You want to know when you'll be able to take your lover to your bed, do you?''

Chela nodded, hating Kohl, knowing it showed.

"Two weeks. Maybe. Maybe a month.''

"That's too long!" Chela moved restlessly in her recliner but didn't allow her eyes to hide from Kohl's stare. If she wasn't very, very careful now, the men could overpower her. Was her father capable of that? "I'm not paying you to stall.''

"You haven't paid me anything yet," he pointed out.

"And I won't until I know when Ortez will be in the country.''

"These things take time," Kohl started, and then, as if he'd grown tired of his own game, he shrugged. "I can have him here in ten days. That's my end of the bargain. Now for yours.''

Chela waited.

"Good." He nodded. "You are learning the virtue of patience. Now you will learn about telling the truth. Forgive me if I'm still suspicious. You have had nothing but hate for me from the beginning. Forgive me if I wonder if I smell a rat."

"What are you talking about?" Chela asked because she knew Kohl wanted some kind of response from her. "I have the money. What more do you want?"

"Reassurance that you're telling me everything, that I'm not going to come to regret this alliance of ours. You asked why I brought your father. What would happen if Ortez was to learn you aren't an orphan after all, that your father is Lou Dye? Your father's reputation is known even in Mexico. When he comes here, Ortez will learn much, much more from the migrants."

Ortez thought she was an orphan? Magadan must have told him to say that. And now Kohl was twisting it to his advantage, only in a way even he didn't suspect. It wasn't Ortez that Chela was thinking about, it was Magadan. "Ortez has no way of knowing what the name Lou Dye means," Chela stalled.

"Not yet he doesn't. But unless you keep him in your bed all the time, he's going to find out. Do you want your lover to learn that your father is the man who cost more than one hundred Mexicans their jobs, their homes, their reason for coming to this country? Do you want your precious Ortez to hear about the most unscrupulous orchardist to ever do business in the valley?"

Chela cringed. She glanced over at her father, but no emotion touched his sagging face. It didn't matter to him. Nothing of what Lou Dye had done mattered to him. That wasn't important, Chela reminded herself. What was important was concentrating on what Kohl was saying. "You'd tell Ortez that?"

"Ortez and everyone who'll listen. You haven't told anyone who your father is, I know that. You've kept that knowledge to yourself, just as your father has. I've talked to your precious migrants. None of them have any inkling that your father is the man responsible for the worst housing conditions a migrant had to endure here. And, I'll bet, neither do your employers."

Neither does Magadan. Most of all, not Magadan. Chela took a ragged breath. Kohl had her right where he wanted her. It was just as bad as she feared it would be. "What do you want?" she whispered, her eyes on her father's impassive face.

"The wild bird has been caged. Admit it, Chela. I knew it could be done. I always knew I could use what Lou told me one drunken night." His laugh was both savage and victorious. "I don't want you to do anything, at least not yet. All I want from you is your reassurance that you won't double-cross me. I want half of that money now and the other half in ten days. Do you understand what happens if you don't do that?"

Chela nodded. She had never felt more like killing another human being, had never felt more defeated. "I have the money," she managed. "Do you want it now?"

"That's right, my little wild bird. How does your cage feel? Tight? Good. I can make it much tighter, squeeze the life out of you, if necessary. Now, get me the money."

Chela found her feet. She stepped past her father

without looking at him and padded into the bedroom. It was somehow fitting that she was barefoot: Slave owners kept their slaves barefoot so they couldn't run off. Chela's captive state wasn't because she didn't have shoes. If Kohl made good on his threat to reveal her parentage—something he was completely capable of—Magadan would find out.

He would know that she was the daughter of a man whose ruthlessness equaled Kohl's.

The envelope was in her middle dresser drawer. As she drew it out, she sensed something of the essence of the man who'd given it to her. If only Magadan were here now!

But that couldn't happen. He'd hear what was being said, look at Lou Dye and know that in her veins flowed the same blood as a man who had left more than one hundred migrants to starve. What would he think of a woman like that?

Chela wasn't going to risk that.

She returned to the living room with the envelope stuffed with money in her numb fingers. She handed it to Kohl without saying a word and sank back into her recliner, trapped. Her father was hand in glove with this man just as he'd been when he was a powerful man in the valley. Kohl was capable of anything, any lie to further himself. Why should she expect her father to be any different?

Finally she lifted her head and faced her father. "If he goes through with his threat, you'll have to acknowledge me as your daughter. Do you want people to know you were once married to a Mexican?"

"Do you think anyone cares?" Lou asked tonelessly.

"I'm dirt here, the lowest snake there is. No one cares about my past."

Chela cared. She had to live with the consequences. "It was a stupid question, wasn't it?" she said savagely. "You never cared that you had a daughter before, so why should I expect it to be any different now?"

"Please." Kohl waved skinny fingers and the envelope in Chela's face. "Let's don't have any more of this touching reunion. What matters is that you understand the options I've given you. You deal with me like a businesswoman, and no one needs to know anything about your father. Double-cross me and you'll have to slink out of this valley with your tail between your legs."

"I understand," Chela managed. Now that his ultimatum had sunk in, she was less shocked by it. She hadn't had time to come to grips with it. That would have to wait for later.

"I thought so. You're no fool, Chela. In fact you'll probably survive much better than your father has. At least you aren't plagued by his arrogance, his greed. That's what caught up with him."

If Chela hadn't been numb, she might have agreed. Arrogance had always been the key to her father's personality. He thought that money gave him the right to be as ruthless as he deemed necessary to build upon that wealth. It took a long, long time for his downfall to take place, because he had money behind him. When it did, he took a lot of innocent people with him.

Chela waited. There was nothing more to say. She was in no mood to continue any kind of conversation. The only thing she wanted was for the two men to leave. She was aware that Kohl was staring at her in obvious glee, relishing his mastery over her. But that didn't affect her nearly as much as the way her father's eyes kept skidding off her face instead of making honest contact. What was he feeling? In a curious sort of way, Chela would have liked to ask him that.

"Aren't you going to kiss your daughter good-bye, Lou?" Kohl asked with a false innocence that was sickening. "I brought about this touching reunion, and you've hardly spoken to your daughter."

Lou rose. "Let's get out of here. There's nothing more to be said."

Kohl laughed. "You're right, there is nothing more to be said. Do you find that sad, Chela? Your father came back to the valley to see you, at my request, and the two of you are still strangers."

"We'll always be strangers," Chela said, taking small pleasure in the punishing words. "We've never been anything else. Why should it change now?"

"You don't understand," Lou broke in. "Your mother and I, we were worlds apart. She wanted nothing to do with my life. She wanted to be with her people."

"So you threw her out of your life," Chela accused, standing so she wouldn't have to look up at the man. "She had your child, but that didn't mean you had any responsibility toward us. No, don't say anything." Chela held up a restraining hand. "I don't want to talk about it any more than you do. Being my father was just as much an accident for you as it was for me. I don't want any more to do with you than you want with me."

"Your mother was never that bitter."

"My mother was too busy trying to raise me," Chela spat. "After all, she had to do it with no help from her husband. She had no skills to take her out of the orchards." She could have said more, make Lou Dye listen to her talk about how the orchards had stripped a fragile woman first of her beauty and then her life. But if Chela did that, she might start crying, and she'd never let her father or Kohl see her cry.

"You're right, Chela," her father sighed. "She wasn't much more than a child when we were married, but then neither was I. I didn't know how to make her happy."

"Enough!" Kohl interrupted. "It's the present we came to talk about, not ancient history."

"I'm aware of that," Lou said, turning on him with anger Chela couldn't fathom. Lou turned back toward his daughter. "Don't try to cross him. That's what I'm here to tell you. You'll regret it."

Chela could almost reach out and finger the vise that tightened around her heart as she watched the two men head for the door. She had to clench her fingers to keep from attacking them, but clench them she did. Chela might indeed be a wild bird trapped in a cage, but she wouldn't let her captors have the satisfaction of watching her struggles.

She made herself wait for the sound of the car pulling out of the driveway and then reached for the telephone. Magadan answered on the first ring. "They just left," Chela blurted out, the words reaching Magadan before she could bring them back.

"They? Who was with Kohl?"

"No one. A partner of his." Chela shut her eyes,

praying Magadan would believe what she was saying. "I can't stay here," she whispered, feeling her father in the room. "Magadan, can I come to your place?"

A pause. "No, Chela, I can't let that happen. I'll be there in five minutes."

Chapter Nine

Chela was sitting outside on the porch when Magadan arrived. She'd tried to make herself stay inside, but her father's unrelenting image was everywhere. Chela hadn't realized that seeing him would be that upsetting. She felt a little like an accident victim trying to assess her injuries. On top of that was the reoccurring thought that he'd tried to warn her, as if he had some feeling for her. It didn't make sense. Magadan would look at her and know she'd been deeply affected by something, but he had no way of knowing her father was around, let alone Lou's connection with Kohl. Let him think her distracted state had been caused by the latter.

Let him think anything he wanted to, she thought as his car pulled into her drive. He still wouldn't tell her where he lived. Didn't that entitle her to some privacy of her own?

Magadan didn't speak. The feeling that crawled up his throat and set his heart to pounding made words impossible. He'd been impressed by Chela's independence, her courage. Now he was looking at a wounded creature who might slip away to suffer in silence if his approach was wrong. Slowly, carefully, he walked up to her, dropped to his knees in front of her and took her icy fingers. Another woman would have collapsed in his arms, but not, he knew, this woman. Somehow he had to find the patience to wait until she was ready to explain the pain in her eyes. For a moment he simply ran his own warm hands from her palm to the tip of her nails until some warmth had been restored to her. "You want to talk about it?" he asked.

Chela shook her head. "I want to get out of here. I can't go to your place, so I don't suppose it matters where I go."

She thought she heard a groan from Magadan's lips. Before she had time to think about it, he was pulling her to her feet and pressing her against him. "I have an idea. Will you go inside for a few minutes? I want to make a phone call, and there's something I want you to do."

Chela didn't object. For once she was willing to let someone else make the decisions. The house seemed less threatening with Magadan in it. She was able to stand apart from him as he dialed and then asked for a dinner reservation for later that evening. "I promised you that lobster dinner," he said as he hung up. "What if you go get dressed? I'll stand sentry to make sure nothing happens."

"You?" Chela almost laughed. "Maybe it's you I need protection from."

"Never. I'd never do anything to hurt you. Go on. Please put on the dress."

Because the day had already carried too many surprises, Chela found nothing strange about what was taking place now. She was still hurt and angry because Magadan kept some part of himself separate from her, but now wasn't the time to think about that. She reached the bathroom door and then turned around. "What are you going to wear?"

He winked. "I always carry a spare suit in the space behind the pickup seat. I wear many hats during the course of a day. I have to be prepared."

Chela was satisfied with that simple explanation. She, maybe more than anyone else, was aware of the multitude of roles Magadan played. That he kept costume changes in his truck came as no surprise.

Because she felt a need to remove any lingering residue of Kohl's touch, Chela spent several minutes in the tub scrubbing her skin vigorously. If only there was an effective way to cleanse her mind and eyes of what they'd experienced today. For the first time she applied a little of the perfume the migrant education staff had given her for her last birthday. The scent cleared her nostrils of the memory of sweat and tobacco and left her renewed. Chela even took time to braid a small section of hair and let it drape down over her ear so she wouldn't have to be constantly brushing her hair out of her eyes. She located her thinnest bra so no seams would show under her dress and slipped on the soft, sensuous peach fabric.

When Chela looked at herself in the mirror, she had to admit that the transformation was complete. Only her too-big eyes gave away anything of what she'd gone through today. Her slim body was the perfect frame for the clinging dress. Her dark coloring highlighted the changing hues in the skirt. Her broad shoulders and firm breasts gave definition to the crossed bodice. Just before leaving the bedroom, Chela applied a light touch of gloss lipstick.

Magadan had changed into his suit while she was in the bathroom. As she was recording the striking way his dark blue suit followed every inch of his frame, he was taking her in with his eyes, his breath. "You look nice," Chela said uncomfortably as she became aware of his unrelenting gaze.

"And you look like a dream. My God. I may have to beat the men off with a club."

Chela ducked her head, blushing. "Don't say that. I'm nervous."

"Why would you be nervous?" Magadan held out his hands but only held her loosely when she came toward him.

"I don't know." She shook her head, her just-washed hair bouncing on her shoulders. "I've never been dressed up like this before. I feel like a character in a play."

"If that's the case, then I want to be the only member of the audience." He brought his nose to the side of her neck. "Perfume. I was going to buy you some."

"You don't have to," she said, feeling shy. "I—I was given some."

"I want to. It wasn't a man, was it?"

Chela thought of her proper supervisor and the two older female members of the migrant education support staff. "Not unless you count a man old enough to be my father." She fought her way around the comparison and continued. "I hope I don't trip. I'm not used to heels like this."

"That's why ladies take the arm of their escorts: So they don't trip and hurt themselves."

Chela laughed, grateful for Magadan's light mood. "I've wondered about that."

"I didn't think I'd hear you laugh. It sounds good. Chela, when I saw you sitting there, I thought you looked as if you'd been hit between the eyes by a board. My mission tonight is to take away that look." His wink lightened the mood. "If I don't get sidetracked by thinking about how much I want to take you to bed."

Magadan's male scent, accented by his suit, made him more sensual than she thought a man should be. But Magadan's talk of lobster dinners, coupled with her outfit, was pulling her in another direction. It was the memory of what she'd gone through in this room not long ago that tipped the scale. "Are we going to be late?"

"The lady isn't going to take me up on my proposition? Ah, Chela, what am I going to do with you? I have the feeling this is going to be a very expensive evening."

"Oh, I didn't think about that—" she started.

"Then don't. You need this tonight. It's something I want to do for you."

Chela nodded and smiled gratefully. She relished the protective way he steered her out of her house by placing his hand in the small of her back. She waited while he locked the door behind her and then guided her to his car, a gentleman taking his date out for a night on the town.

Chela didn't look back. Thinking about the meeting

with Kohl and her father, let alone telling Magadan about it, was the last thing she wanted to do. Maybe Magadan didn't trust her enough to let her see where he lived. At least he was perceptive enough to sense how much she needed what they were doing now.

Magadan explained the restaurant's decor as he drove. The Bella Mansion had been built during pioneer days to house the town's first banker. It continued in use as a home for several decades, but eventually no single family could afford the many rooms and extensive grounds. It had been converted into a restaurant over thirty years ago and remained in the same hands since then. "The cook has been to schools in Europe and treats each dish as if it's his own personal masterpiece. There's no comparison between it and the hamburger stand we went to. Or the Blue Max for that matter. This is true elegance."

Chela had been past the Bella Mansion many times and marveled at the spreading oak trees standing sentry over the extensive parking area. She'd glimpsed some of the two-story mansion from the road, but the one-hundred-year-old-plus trees hid most of the structure. Although it wasn't quite dark, there were already hanging lanterns lit to welcome dinner guests. Chela barely controlled a gasp as they walked up the broad expanse of stairs and past two magnificent statues of stags.

They stepped inside and waited a moment while their eyes adjusted to the muted lighting. Despite herself Chela leaned toward Magadan, fighting off an urge to turn and flee. What was she doing here? The cavernous room stretching ahead of them was dominated by a large circular fireplace in the center of the room.

Flanking the fireplace were intimate tables for couples wishing a cocktail before dinner. An arched doorway in the distance led, Chela believed, to the dining room.

Magadan leaned toward her. "Are you okay?"

Chela blinked back tears. So this was what she and her mother had never experienced. Her father had been here, she was sure of it.

No! She wasn't going to think about that. Magadan had brought her here so she could forget her father. "I'm all right," she whispered, trembling a little. "I—I guess I just didn't think it'd be like another world."

"It is that I guess," Magadan acknowledged. "But all of us need a little fantasy once in a while. Please let me indulge you."

With Magadan's presence to give her courage, Chela allowed herself to be led into the room. The thick carpet cushioned her steps and increased the feeling that she'd stepped into another world. She was grateful when he pulled out a chair and settled her at one of the small tables to the left of the fireplace. "We have a little time before dinner," Magadan said as he took the chair opposite hers. "I'd like to order you a drink."

Chela nodded. It was hard to believe she had really spent the day sweating in the orchards. She wondered if this was her escape from her first face-to-face meeting with her father in years. Magadan was right. The Bella Mansion was for fantasies. She focused on Magadan, using him as her passport out of reality. His voice was more rumble than sound as he placed an order. His hand over hers across the table was a soft blanket. "You are beautiful," he whispered, his eyes shining despite the dark interior broken only by candles at each table. "The most beautiful woman in this room."

"I'm a migrant teacher, although I don't feel much like one tonight."

Unexpectedly Magadan lifted her hand and brought it to his lips. "You don't look much like a migrant teacher tonight. Just be what I see, a beautiful woman."

What Magadan was saying filled Chela's mind. There was no denying that she'd thought of the differences between them many times. But tonight they were locked together in an environment that made no such distinction. "I don't know what we are to each other anymore, Magadan," she said softly after the waitress had placed the cool glass of white wine in front of her. "Every time I think I know, things change."

"That's because we're changing. I thought you were beautiful, unique, from the moment I met you. But I didn't know you then."

"Do you now?" Chela took a sip and challenged him. "Do you know who I am, Magadan?"

He shook his head. "No, but I think I'm learning. I want to learn everything about you. Like—" He paused a moment as if hesitant to continue. "Like what happened this afternoon. It wasn't just Kohl. Something else happened."

An hour ago Chela might have fled or at least closed herself off from his question, but the atmosphere had blunted her reactions, made her less skittish. "Something else happened, but I can't tell you what it was. Not now and maybe never. Please. You have to accept that."

For a moment Magadan's eyes sought to pierce her defense. "All right," he sighed. "I don't have any choice, do I?"

Chela shook her head, unaware that the movement caused a couple of men to pause in their conversations and stare at the striking, raven-haired young woman. "Just as I have no choice when you close certain doors to me."

"I don't like it having to be like that," Magadan admitted. "I'd like to tell you everything there is to tell about me but—" His eyes narrowed. "Tonight feels good. I don't want to risk anything."

"Neither do I," Chela admitted, smiling. As the cool wine warmed her veins and blunted even more her usual world, Chela told Magadan what she could of her latest contact with Kohl. Despite her continued suspicions of the coyote, she honestly believed he would follow through with his plans to relieve her, or Magadan rather, of the money they were dangling in front of him. She was equally sure that Ortez wouldn't be delivered to her until Kohl had drained her of every cent he could. He relished playing cat and mouse. "It could be dangerous for Ortez," she pointed out.

"He's aware of that. But Ortez dislikes the man as much as you do. He's willing to take certain risks. I'm a lot more concerned about the risks to you."

"I'm not afraid of Kohl."

"Aren't you?" Magadan had been lounging against the back of his chair as she talked, but now he leaned forward. "Something made you look like a deer about to bolt."

"I didn't bolt," she pointed out. "I'm still here."

"Will you be able to say that if the man with Kohl, whoever he is, comes back again?"

Chela glanced around the room, desperately seeking the illusions that were keeping her insulated from reality. "Let me worry about that, Magadan," she said as their waitress approached. "I'm not asking you to fight my battles for me."

Chela let Magadan take her hand as they walked from the cocktail room into the main dining hall. She distracted herself by studying the red linen tablecloths draped over tables decorated with fresh flowers and candles. She marveled at the attire of their fellow diners, not realizing that even the women were looking her way. Heavy red draperies covered the windows and the same thick carpet silenced the sound of footsteps. It seemed to Chela that everyone in the room was whispering. For some reason that made her want to laugh.

She tried to concentrate on the menu, but she'd never heard of most of the dishes and the prices quite overwhelmed her. Finally she turned the decision-making over to Magadan. "Does it show? Do I look like a bull in a china shop?"

"Hardly." He pointed out the lobster dish and placed their order with the waitress. "You're doing very well here."

Chela sighed. "My foster parents were very proper. They made sure I learned table manners. They tried to instruct me in the art of small talk, but I never saw a reason for it."

"Were you at all close to your foster parents?" Magadan asked, his eyes never leaving her face. "It doesn't seem right that you should be so alone after your mother died."

Chela jerked her head up. "No. I never felt close to my foster parents. They believed it was their duty to provide for some of the world's unfortunates. I don't think it ever occurred to them that those unfortunates needed love." Chela shook her head angrily. "I'm sorry. I didn't mean to say that. I haven't thought about that part of my life for a long time."

"I didn't mean to stir it up. I just want to know more about you. I'm going to keep asking questions like that until I get the answers I want."

"I don't think so, Magadan," Chela challenged. "You don't give me certain answers. Why should I be the only one?"

Magadan's eyes darkened until they resembled caves. "There's no arguing that and you know it. Damn! We make life complicated for ourselves, don't we?"

Chela's eyes widened as their waitress brought a carafe of wine and placed it between them. She didn't remember Magadan ordering that. "Life's complicated. More so than I want to think about. Are you trying to get me drunk?"

"Hardly. I think you'd stop before you got to that point. But you need to relax tonight. I want to make sure that happens." Magadan poured twin glasses and handed one to her. He sounded like a tour guide as he explained that the wine came from a local vineyard, which, although small, made excellent dry white wines.

"How do you know so much about local wines?" Chela asked absently as she took a sip. Magadan was right. The wine slid like velvet down her throat.

"I could tell you I have inside information on such things, but the truth is there was an article on the vineyard in the newspaper's business section a few weeks ago. So much for impressing you with my expertise."

Chela tried to digest that bit of information, but the wine had done its work. She was a lot more interested in dinner and people-watching than trying to dig through the layers to the real Magadan.

It was dark by the time Chela and Magadan left the restaurant, but people were still arriving. "It's nine," she observed. "How can they wait so long to eat?"

"Probably because they don't have breakfast at 6:00 A.M. How did you like the lobster? I got to thinking, maybe it was too rich for you."

"I'll tell you in the morning," Chela admitted as she slid her arm around Magadan's waist in response to his arm around her. "Tonight was special. The dinner was the most perfect meal of my life."

"I think you should tell the chef. He'd probably serve you for nothing from now on. It was a good evening, wasn't it?" Magadan started to open the truck door but wound up taking Chela in his arms instead. Overhead one of the lanterns cast a romantic glow on the two caught in an embrace that took them beyond the Bella Mansion parking lot.

Chela felt herself swaying in Magadan's grasp, but she knew she was in no danger of losing her footing. So women held on to their escorts' arms to keep from tottering on their high heels? In Chela's case her precarious stance came, not from her shoes, but her reaction to a kiss that seemed to hold no dimension of time. It wasn't just the wine, or the effects of a magnificent dinner.

Her state came from knowing that what had happened earlier in her house was a world removed from what she was experiencing now. Moths flitted around the lanterns. Night was cooling the summer-sun-heated day. The scent of roses from trailing vines around the restaurant piqued Chela's nostrils and made her aware of her heightened sensual response to everything. Her bare arms felt the breeze, her ears caught the whisper of moving wings from the moths, but the real, overriding response came from what Magadan's lips were doing to her entire body.

Chela questioned if she existed as a separate person now or if her essence had been interwoven with Magadan's. She wondered how she had gone this far in life without knowing that this emotion was possible.

I think I love you, Magadan. I think that's what's happening. Chela gripped Magadan's neck tightly, her revelation making her dizzy.

"Do you know what I wish?" Magadan whispered. "I wish tonight would never end."

"You do? That's a beautiful thought."

Magadan kissed her lightly on the nose. "I have an even more interesting thought. Do you know what I'd like to do? I've never walked through an orchard at night."

"There's a mystery to it," Chela supplied as she slid into her side of the truck. "There are sounds all around, but you can't tell where they're coming from. You can smell the heat in the ground, even when the air's cool. You can almost feel things growing."

"Do you want to go there?"

The alternative was going back to her place. "Yes. I

don't care where we go. Why don't you try Walker Road? There are orchards there with histories that go back nearly a century." Chela placed her head on Magadan's shoulder as he started the engine. So this was what it was like to be protected, to have someone take over. It wasn't bad.

Chela might have dozed, she wasn't sure. She didn't really become aware of her surroundings until they'd been traveling for half an hour. She rubbed her eyes, sat up. Walker Road had narrowed down until there was no longer any shoulder. They were far from the city limits—and closing in on her past.

"Here," Chela directed, surprised to hear the word come from her mouth. "Please pull over here."

"Are you sure?"

"You wanted to walk through an orchard at night." Chela took a deep breath to still the warning voice inside her. Magadan was with her. She was safe. She could touch base with her past. "There are things...I haven't been here for two years."

Magadan gave her a look she took to mean he sought a further explanation, but instead of giving it, she slipped out of the truck and waited for him to join her. The sounds and smells here were no different from any other orchard. She could take Magadan's arm, tell him what she dared about the land. "The nearest house is two miles away," she said softly, gaining courage. "The only building around is a storage shed for the equipment."

It wasn't the orchard's fault that her father had once owned it. There were some thirty acres of Comice pears sheltered from much of spring's frost by their secluded location between two low hills. The pears here might not be the first to ripen in the fall, but they were less likely to be damaged by freezing temperatures. "It's one of the few orchards still to use smudge pots," she remembered aloud. The pots, which contained oil, were fired in the spring to protect fragile buds from frost. "The—the former owner didn't put much money in it."

"Look," Magadan said. "Can you see the overhead sprinklers?"

Chela couldn't make out the high, thin metal pipes rising above the trees, but it didn't surprise her that she didn't know about the improvements. She had avoided all talk about Hidden Valley Orchard. "An ice coating on the buds does a much better job of protection from frost," she explained. "A lot has changed here. I wonder what else the current owner has been doing."

"Do you want to find out?" Magadan's eyes were on her but unreadable in the dark.

Chela leaned over and removed her shoes. She started across the ditch in her stockinged feet before answering. "I think I do now."

He followed her. They walked side by side down the open space between the two rows of trees, not touching, silence settling comfortably over them. Chela was thinking about the sounds night birds made and what the wild asparagus growing at the foot of the trees tasted like. The orchard hadn't been watered in the last day or two, which meant she didn't have to worry about sinking into mud. The carpet of grass under her feet kept her stockings from being ruined, but she wouldn't mind even if they were. Stockings were things she wore when she slipped into a fancy dress and went off to a fantasy mansion for dinner. They had nothing to do with her real world.

"The pears look as if they'll be ready in about two months," Magadan observed, breaking a silence that had gone on for almost five minutes. "For fall pears they're ripening fast in the hot weather. I'm glad to see that. The dry cycle a few years ago was hard on the crop."

Chela stopped and turned toward him. Not many people concerned themselves with the weather's influence on the pear harvest. "You know what happened here?"

"Of course. I'm a businessman. I also know that during the years when this orchard wasn't being properly maintained, there was substantial damage due to insects. That's the best damn way I know of losing it all. Spraying isn't a luxury, it's a necessity."

"You know about... the man who used to own this place?"

"I didn't move here until things had gone sour for him." Magadan placed his hands on Chela's shoulders and held her firmly. "I don't want to talk about that, do you?"

Chela dropped her head and muttered an anguished, "No." She'd hidden from this all evening, but now was the time to face what Kohl had thrown in her face. Magadan couldn't know about it, but he was talking about her father. Lou Dye was the man whose greed had allowed an orchard to become neglected and unproductive, who failed to inform seasonal workers of this until they'd already come here. How many workers had Lou Dye, her father, lied to? But that wasn't all her father had done.

She couldn't tell Magadan that. Up until a few weeks ago she'd kept her secret because she wanted to keep buried something that belonged in the past. Back then, her father's identity was none of Magadan's business. Now, however, her closed lips and clenched teeth were caused by something else.

A woman falling in love didn't drag skeletons out of the closet when she wondered if, for the first time in her life, maybe she wasn't going to be alone anymore. Maybe Magadan kept things from her, but tonight she wasn't going to question that. What she had to realize was that as a businessman Magadan was aware of the extent of Lou Dye's ruthlessness. What would it do to Magadan's feelings for her if he knew Lou's blood ran in her veins?

No, Chela told herself. That was her secret. Her father made a lie of everything she believed in. She hadn't been able to reconcile that in her own heart; she couldn't find words of explanation for Magadan.

"You're quiet," he said as he released her shoulders and took her hand.

Chela started to answer, but something about his hand stopped her. His fingers were cold, and he was gripping her so tightly that it was painful. "Am I?" was the best she could offer.

"You were thinking about something," Magadan said, his voice deeper than she remembered it being. "Will you share it with me?"

"No," Chela said. She knew she heard the quick escape of Magadan's breath.

Again they walked in silence, closer this time because their fingers were locked around each other. Chela tried to make her thoughts go back to her surroundings, but they wouldn't leave the ramification of conversations toyed with, touched, and then put back in hiding. Secrets were more blinding than any night.

Suddenly Magadan stopped. He whirled on her and brought her fiercely into the circle of his arms. "God, you feel so good!"

What's wrong? Chela asked inside, alarmed. *What are you thinking, Magadan?* But she didn't ask the questions pulsing through her. Instead she surrendered herself to the man's strength. She felt small and fragile and vulnerable in her stockinged feet and delicate dress with the top that allowed the night air to toy with the swell of her breasts. The woman who clung to Magadan wasn't the one who trod through the orchards. She felt like one of the women she'd observed from afar but never thought she'd understand. It took more than a hand placed on a man's arm to make a woman feel protected. It took a body that blocked out the world, quick breaths on her hair, a masculine chest beating against hers.

Suddenly hungry, Chela groped for Magadan's neck and drew him down to her aching lips. His mouth was both gentle and commanding, touching and satisfying some nerve, some aching essence that had hurt so long Chela didn't know there was any other way to feel.

Tonight she understood that there was an alternative to loneliness. She wasn't alone anymore. The orchard had always been Chela's friend. She'd been content to share it with Spanish-speaking migrants, quick-learning children, even Anglo foremen. But that brand of sharing wasn't anything like what was happening tonight.

Tonight Chela realized that the orchards had insulated her from what was washing over her, threatening to throw her to her knees when she least expected it. The orchard was her friend, it wasn't her lover. There lay the difference.

And Chela needed a lover, a man to sense the source of the hungry, aching cry within her and satisfy that cry. She needed arms around her, lips caressing hers. Tonight, at least, Magadan was that man.

"I'm going to make love to you, Chela. Here." Magadan kissed her again, a kiss that stripped away everything else. He left her alone, holding on to a branch for support while he went into the supply shed. A moment later he returned with a blanket tucked under his arm. Chela studied his dark outline as he shook out the blanket and spread it on the ground between two trees, then he took her in his arms. "It can be good for us, Chela. Better than anything either of us has had before."

Only honesty could make it better was the thought that sliced through Chela's mind. Quickly it escaped into the night and was lost.

"I'm shaking," she admitted, clinging to him. "Why?"

"So am I," he laughed. "I don't think either of us knew this was going to happen."

Chela didn't ask him if he was talking about tonight or something larger. Instead she found the buttons on his suit jacket and undid them. She draped the jacket over the tree branch she'd used to support herself earlier and then turned to his tie.

"I hate those things," he said when she gave up trying to figure out how it was knotted. "It's a costume I can do without."

"How many costumes do you have? Who is the real you?" Suddenly she stopped him with a hand on his mouth. "Don't answer that tonight."

Magadan had action, not words, on his mind. Chela was fascinated by the sure way he was able to undo her belt and pull the dress over her head without tangling her hair. He unfastened her bra without making her turn away from him. He removed both her panty hose and underpants before taking her in his arms again.

"We keep winding up like this, don't we?" he whispered against her ear. "No matter what happens, we wind up in each other's arms."

That's because it's the only place I want to be, Chela thought, but she didn't say the words aloud because she knew that they represented too much of a surrender. What was happening between them was still too new. Things could happen at any moment to shatter their fragile relationship. All she could ask for was perfection tonight.

Magadan seemed to share her thoughts. He undressed and pulled her down onto the blanket with him. He wasn't in a hurry; instead he seemed to need to explore her body, commit her outline to memory.

Chela shut her eyes, completing the darkness that the night had begun. She held on to Magadan with hungry fingers and locked her lips over the animal moans that built every time he explored a new inch of flesh. Her breasts, shoulders, waist, stomach, no longer belonged to her. They were now part of Magadan, claimed by strong warm fingers that made her as willing as a newborn kitten.

But no kitten felt the sensations Chela was feeling. When he kissed her, she could no longer deny the sounds inside. Her deep groan, accompanied by her spine arching toward him, told him everything he needed to know. She was his. Completely.

"You do things to me," he whispered. "Things that scare me."

Magadan was scared? That seemed odd, Chela thought; the man was always in control, wasn't he?

She didn't have time to answer her question, though. She was in the act of surrender; that was the only thing that had any meaning. She wanted, needed Magadan. Her hungry body sought his under the dark sentry of pear trees. The ground accepted the twin weights of their bodies joined by lovemaking.

No human was within miles to observe what was taking place. And the night creatures who watched kept well their secrets.

Chapter Ten

Chela stayed away from Hidden Valley Orchard until midafternoon. She had no reason to return to the scene of last night's lovemaking, but something, some kind of force, drew her there. Despite the glow that remained with her after Magadan brought her home, Chela slept little and went through the day restless and upset. Being with Magadan had been able to erase, for the space of several perfect hours, the meeting with her father.

In the reality of day, Chela realized there were things that couldn't be denied. Last night, in Hidden Valley Orchard, she had touched base with the past. It was here that her father's roots remained. Right or wrong, she had to learn how much of herself was there as well.

The orchard looked even better by day than it had at night. The two years during which Chela couldn't bring herself to come here had been kind to the trees. Although work still needed to be done, trimming and the installation of both an effective watering system and overhead sprinklers resulted in trees that now bore enough fruit to rival competitive orchards.

Whoever had taken over the orchard once her father's bankruptcy was settled hadn't wasted time or money bringing the orchard back into the mainstream of cultivation. But that wasn't Chela's concern. She needed to know what it had been like when her father had owned the orchard. If the rumors of his total disregard for workers' rights and welfare were as blatant as she believed. If he had really been so unfeeling as to ignore the health department's regulations regarding water and sanitary facilities at the adjacent barrio.

It seemed impossible that the man, who was despite it all her father, could have believed he could continue to fly in the face of authority, refuse to pay his bills, cheat his employees. Those rumors had grown and persisted until they were accepted as fact; even Chela didn't try to deny their validity. What she needed to learn, if possible, was why.

She hardly believed she'd find any workers who'd been here two years ago, but maybe those who lived and worked here now carried the thread of the story. Maybe they knew how much the new owner had done, how much damage he'd had to undo.

Pedro Cruz, who was the foreman here but came to another orchard to take English writing classes, might supply at least some of the answers. The sunbaked older Mexican had lived here as a legal for enough years to understand the politics and power plays that took place in the pear industry. In fact Pedro had been here long enough to have known Chela's mother. His was the only name in authority she'd heard connected with Hidden Valley Orchard.

Chela found Pedro working with a section of irrigation pipe near the supply shed less than thirty feet from where she and Magadan had made love last night. The man's face threatened to crack into a thousand tiny splinters when Chela called out to him.

"I thought you said it was too far out here for you to drive," Pedro said in his practiced English. "Have you come here to dig ditches with me?"

Chela laughed away Pedro's challenge. She wanted to touch his dry, leathery face to return natural oils to it, but to do so would take away Pedro's character and the proof of how he earned his living. "I heard the orchard was back in production," she said casually. "I came to see for myself."

"Let me finish with this," Pedro said. "I'll take you on the tour. It isn't what it was before."

Chela squatted beside Pedro and watched silently as he rethreaded fittings on the thick white plastic hose, his small, powerful hands doing what she would have needed a wrench for. As long as she'd been coming to the orchards, she never grew tired of watching men giving their days in service to trees and the fruit they bore. "Is your son going back to school in the fall?" she asked. "He has magic in his hands like you do, but his brain— He asks questions I can't answer."

Pedro looked up at her. His mouth cracked into a smile, but his eyes were deep and serious. "Pascual has a scholarship. Can you believe that? My son took a computer course and now he has a scholarship."

Chela blinked rapidly and rose to her feet. Pascual with his straight back and questioning eyes wouldn't spend his life in the orchards. Someone, probably his computer teacher, had discovered his quick mind.

"Keep him in school, Pedro," she said, knowing she sounded like a teacher.

"It's a promise he already made. Come now. I want to get this pipe back in so we can water tonight. Pascual is going to be an aide at the high school's Spanish class. You taught him English, and now he's teaching Spanish to Anglos."

Chela walked beside Pedro, sharing his pride. It was the same kind of feeling she was starting to have for the orchard. Pedro would never know that her father had been responsible for Hidden Valley Orchard's downfall. She could nod at his enthusiasm for what was happening to it now, share that with him. Unless Kohl made good on his threat to expose her.

Chela jerked away from the thought and concentrated on what Pedro was telling her. The orchard, which was one of the larger ones in the valley, still hadn't come back up to full production, but rot had been removed from the trees. In the fall some of the older trees would be removed to make room for new seedlings.

"It's costing thousands," Chela observed when Pedro was through reconnecting the plastic pipe. They stood and gazed down an endless row, where in the distance a jackrabbit stared back at them. "The new owner must be a rich man."

"He doesn't say much about himself," Pedro explained. "When he first came, he didn't have much knowledge of orchards. I thought that kind of man would take over a business he knows nothing about only if he has confidence in himself. He learns fast. He listens to what I tell him about what needs to be done and brings in biologists and people from the extension service. The man isn't like many orchardists." Pedro turned away from the rabbit and faced her. "He has great respect for migrants. He speaks their language. He tore down the old housing and put in cabins with running water and inside toilets. He made the health department very happy."

"Then he must be rich," Chela repeated.

Pedro smiled. "You know what he tells me? He says he was able to buy the orchard for almost nothing because of the bankruptcy. He says he was there to take advantage of Lou Dye's misfortune. The land cost him little. That's why he can spend money on improvements."

A chill touched Chela. Lou Dye—there was no escaping the name. "Does he say much about Lou, about why so many things went wrong when Lou Dye was the orchardist?"

Pedro shook his head. "Joe Magadan talks about today and tomorrow, not yesterday."

For the space of a breath Chela thought she was going to scream. Magadan! The new owner was Magadan!

"Are—are you sure that's who it is?" Chela asked stupidly. Her legs, arms, everything, turned numb.

"You know him?" Pedro asked.

Chela nodded. "Oh, yes, I know this Magadan. Or I thought I did."

"There aren't many Anglos like him," Pedro was saying. "He doesn't make mistakes that the migrants pay for with lost wages. He doesn't call the immigration officers for a raid when it's time to pay his workers. He says he doesn't care whether a migrant is legal or illegal, just whether he does his work and has a place to live."

Chela couldn't concentrate on what Pedro was telling her. Magadan had kept secrets from her. This was it. But why?

The answers weren't in the orchard. She couldn't ask Pedro why a man, her lover, wouldn't tell her what he did for a living. There was only one person who could tell her the truth.

Pedro must have wondered at Chela's sudden departure, but she was too upset to find the words to explain away the glazed look in her eyes and the trembling in her fingers. She knew she shouldn't be driving, but her need for answers was greater than her sense of caution. She wanted to get away from Hidden Valley Orchard, find Magadan.

And, now, she thought she knew where to find him.

So Magadan had taken over her father's orchard. He had probably taken over the grand house in the east hills as well—that was why he'd never wanted her to come there.

By the time Chela reached the house she hoped to never see again, she was barely able to command enough strength to keep her foot on the gas pedal. She pulled off to the side of the street and got out, aware of the contrast her battered, dusty Jeep made with the expensive cars parked behind shrub and fence-lined property lines. She could have pulled into the driveway herself, but because she'd never wanted to claim the two-story, shake-roofed house with its swimming pool and sauna, she didn't.

Although there was no sign of life from the house

and Magadan's pickup wasn't in the driveway, she was
sure this was where she'd find him. He now owned her
father's orchard. A businessman would see the advantage of taking over the house involved in the bankruptcy scandal at the same time.

Chela walked along the brick walk until she reached
the step leading to the front door. The house rose
above her like some monster. She took a deep breath
that came out sounding too much like a moan and
reached for the doorbell. The chimes echoed throughout the interior, mocking her. "No one home. You'll
have to wait."

Chela turned around and sat on the step, arms
locked around her upper body, sweating from the heat,
cold within. Magadan might not be home for hours,
but she'd wait. She had no choice.

In the silence that exists in a wealthy neighborhood
with acreage and well-tended trees and hedges separating the houses from each other, Chela tried to come to
grips with the ramifications of what Pedro had said.
There could be many reasons why Magadan didn't
want her to know where he lived or what he did for a
living. Keeping this from her might have been his way
of decreasing the distance between them or deluding
her into believing that they didn't live in opposing
worlds.

It was also possible that in the process of taking over
Lou Dye's holdings, Magadan had learned things about
Lou that no one except Kohl knew. A sudden chill tore
through Chela. Did Magadan know who her father
was?

For two hours Chela's brain pounded with unanswered questions. No matter which direction her tortured mind turned, there were too many questions and not enough answers. That was why she sat, unmoving, as the shadows stretched first across the lawn and then up the walk to touch her legs. If Magadan knew Lou was her father, then he must know how much she hated that fact. Perhaps he was holding his knowledge in reserve to use against her should his lips and arms and body no longer be enough to get her to do what he wanted.

Chela didn't want to believe that. Anything but that.

She didn't move when she heard the pickup pull into the driveway. Magadan, with his probing eyes and masterful hands that were teaching her what it felt like to be a woman, was coming toward her. He seemed to be walking slower than usual.

Finally, when she felt his eyes on her, she looked up, arms still wrapped around her bent knees. Her hair had fallen down around her face. As she lifted her head, her hair clung to her cheeks and collarbone. "I've been waiting for you, Magadan," she said in a voice so lifeless she didn't recognize it.

"I see that. Do you want to come in?"

Chela rose. At least he wasn't lying, trying to tell her that this wasn't his home. "Yes."

She waited while he unlocked the front door and then stepped in ahead of him. He didn't touch her, which saved her. She had no idea what would happen if he'd tried to kiss her. The door opened into a tiled entryway devoid of any furnishings. It wasn't until they'd reached what Chela took to be the living room that she saw any wall decorations. Despite her numb state Chela was able to make out twin paintings of antique cars in thin silver frames. The paintings were little more than stark outlines without warmth or personality. They were, she supposed, expensive but a mystery to Chela. She questioned why a man would want dark sketches of a metal machine when he could afford something with vitality in it. Were they Magadan's or had her father left them behind?

She asked the same questions about the glass-topped coffee table, the chocolate velvet couch and matching chair, the thick, rich carpet beneath her dusty tennis shoes. She wondered how much of her father was still here.

"Can I get you anything to drink, eat?" Magadan asked. She turned to see him standing to the side and behind her, his hands hanging at his sides. He looked defeated.

Although she was thirsty, she shook her head. She didn't want to be beholden to Magadan for anything until he'd been honest with her. She forced a sudden film away from her eyes and located a hardwood end table near the couch. Chela brushed aside the magazines and perched on it. The couch was too expensive for her dirty work clothes.

Chela waited for Magadan to sit on the couch. He was wearing the same boots and jeans she'd seen him in once before. Why hadn't the pieces started to come together then? Magadan had said he wore many costumes in his life. The most telling was the one that said he was at home in an orchard.

"How many orchards do you own?" she asked.

"Three. As of this week. Chela, what's going on?"

Chela lifted her hand in a gesture designed to ward him off. "Not now, Magadan," she said coldly. "Now I'm asking the questions. Why didn't you tell me you own Hidden Valley Orchard?"

"How did you find out?" His eyes were on hers, but their outward calm was being given away by the stiff manner in which he held his body.

"Don't ask me questions." She took a deep breath. "You've had your secrets long enough. Why didn't you tell me?"

"You wouldn't understand."

"You never gave me a chance!" she shot at him. "You never trusted me enough to tell me the truth. I went there today, to where we made love last night." Her voice dropped to a near whisper. "I'm not sure why I was drawn there. Now I wish to God I hadn't."

"Whom did you talk to?"

She allowed him that question. From another room she could hear a large clock ticking. She wanted to talk to cover up the hollow sound in the otherwise silent house. Briefly she told him about meeting his foreman. "At least you did that right," she spat angrily. "Pedro is a loyal man. He loves growing things and he has a quick mind."

"He also has a big mouth! I told him I had to keep a low profile, that no one was to know who bought the orchard. No," Magadan relented when she started to interrupt, "I don't blame Pedro. He had no idea what he was revealing. What did he tell you?"

"Why should I tell you that, Magadan? You wouldn't tell me anything." Chela tried to clamp a lid over her emotions, but it was too late. "He told me that the new owner of the orchard Lou Dye left behind was one Joe Magadan. You have his orchard and his fine house. That's why you didn't want me to know where you lived.''

Magadan sighed and leaned forward. For a long minute his eyes bore into hers as if searching for something he hadn't found. "It's an orchardist's house. I know how you feel about orchardists."

"Oh, yes, the mighty orchardists! They take and take and give nothing in return. Your workers live in cabins while you live in this fine house. I have to sit on the ground with them in the middle of a summer afternoon to give them an education because you and your kind expect them to be nothing more than a means to a greedy end."

"That isn't true, Chela," Magadan countered. "You know that. If you talked to Pedro, then you must know what I've been doing out there."

"It isn't enough!" Chela wasn't going to bend beneath Magadan's anger. Her own fury, spurred on by pain, matched everything he could throw at her. "Pedro, your foreman, still can't write an English letter. He has to come to me for that." She lifted her lips in a cruel smile. "At least Pedro's son has escaped you. He won't die in the orchards."

Magadan was on his feet, looming over her. "People don't die in the orchards."

"My mother did."

Her words seemed to stop him. He stared at her as if struck. "That was a long time ago, Chela," he said softly.

"I haven't forgotten," she said just as softly.

Magadan took a backward step. "What do you want out of me?"

"The truth. Or maybe that's too much to ask." Chela had to dig her nails into her palms to keep her body still. Having Magadan that close was nearly her undoing. No matter what fury raged through her, she still wanted, needed, this man. The end to what they'd begun was agony. "How much did you have to pay for Lou Dye's orchard, and for this house? Did you know his empire was falling down around him? Were you there waiting to attack, a coyote closing in for the kill?"

Magadan seemed to recoil from her accusation. "Does it look like that to you, Chela?"

"It doesn't matter." She shrugged. "This house costs more than I'll make in a lifetime. Do you like living here, Magadan? Do you like being able to come home to this evidence of your power?"

"It's a place to live. Nothing else. Chela, I haven't had time to think about that. I became owner of Hidden Valley Orchard not that long ago. So much had to be done there. Then, there was another orchard, and last week I closed a deal on my third. That—and seeing you—is all there's been time for."

"Not anymore, Magadan," she managed, despite the agony his words caused her. "From now on you'll have all the time you need to increase your empire. Is this a game? Are you trying to see how many orchards you can take over?" She knew she should stop attacking the man, but she hurt and wanted to inflict pain in return. "You say you hate coyotes like Kohl, but aren't you one yourself? You prey on the weakness of other men, wait until you've found their vulnerability, and close in for the kill.''

"Is that what you believe?"

The pain in Magadan's voice almost stopped her, but she struggled on. "Why shouldn't I? Haven't I been one of your victims?"

"You'll never be a victim, Chela," he interrupted.

"Don't tell me what I am!" she shouted, because shouts were better than tears. "Don't forget, I've watched you in action. You came after me and after me, got through to me because you knew how I felt about Kohl. You knew there was danger in your plan, but you kept on with it anyway. And when you sensed I might take the bait, you brought me around by taking advantage of something else."

For once Magadan didn't speak. He was still standing over her, but he hadn't moved in several minutes.

"You were afraid I'd back out, leave you to deal with Kohl on your own, so you found my most vulnerable point." Chela took a ragged breath and fought the tears that were making her eyes glisten. "You knew I was lonely. Like a coyote you sensed my weakness. You offered your body as bait."

"It wasn't like that. It was never like that!"

"Don't lie to me anymore, Magadan!" Chela fairly screamed as she surged off her perch on the end table. "You lied about this house, about the Hidden Valley Orchard. Why should I believe anything you say?"

"Our bodies didn't lie to each other."

Chela whirled away from the truth of Magadan's words. She was too confused, too hurt to be able to deal with what he was saying. Maybe their lovemaking had been good, but that was the work of two bodies, not two minds. The crucial question still hadn't been answered. Did he know Lou Dye was her father? Did he think she condoned anything he did? Maybe he did and that was how he was able to justify what he was doing to her.

"I don't blame you for wanting to live here, Magadan," she said in a voice as cold as death. "Who wouldn't rather live here than in a little house with wooden floors and an ancient bathtub. No wonder you didn't want to share this with me. I belong in my little house, not this mansion. Forgive me for not understanding. You didn't tell me you were an orchardist because I'm not good enough to share your life-style. I was good enough to make love to in an orchard but not in your bed."

"Don't say that, Chela."

"Why not? It's the truth, isn't it?" she mocked. "Anyone would want this grand house." That was a lie, she admitted. It was the last thing she'd ever want. "But it's too good for the dirty little Mexican girl you've been playing with."

"Don't say that!" This time Magadan reinforced his order by grabbing her and holding her so she couldn't escape. "You're not a dirty little Mexican girl. You were never that."

"Then what am I?" she asked, tense and trembling in his grip.

Magadan answered by pulling her hard against him and sealing her lips with his own. He bent her backward and held her arms tight against her side until keeping her balance was all Chela had the strength for.

Despite herself, despite pain and rage, Chela needed to feel his lips against hers. She closed her eyes, desperately trying to block out the words that had been spoken here this afternoon. If only they could go back to those first gentle days when she was learning what it meant to be a woman!

Maybe, for one last minute, she could. Chela stopped struggling and let Magadan support her. It didn't matter if he took her response for surrender. Nothing mattered but those precious, desperate moments when she was aware of nothing but his lips turning from punishment to pleasure on her mouth. His hands still held her arms, but his fingers no longer dug into her tanned, naked flesh. He was strength and warmth and life, everything she'd wanted him to be.

Magadan, I love you! Despite it all, I still love you!

Tears stung Chela's eyes and started pounding a path to her brain. As her headache came to life, she clung even more desperately to this last unreasoning moment with Magadan. He was a secret, private man who didn't trust her enough. He was also her lifeline.

"Don't go, Chela," he whispered. "We can talk it out."

His words ruined the mood. Chela swam back to reality. "About what? It's all been said."

"No it hasn't. I don't want you to hate me."

How can I hate you? Chela cried silently. *I'm a million miles from that. All I feel is pain.* "You aren't what I thought you were," she said as he was placing her back on her feet. "That's enough."

"No it isn't." He still hadn't let go of her. "All right. Maybe I should have told you, but—"

"It's too late for that." She struggled briefly, wanting nothing more than to escape this house, this man. "It's too late for anything."

"I don't believe that. Chela, what about Kohl?"

"I almost forgot," she laughed harshly, her words rasping her aching throat. "We still have an agreement, a contract. There's Kohl to bring to justice. Tell me again. Why do you want to put an end to him?"

"He's a coyote."

"Like you!" Chela's fury was back full strength. "You have your magnificent new den," she taunted, whipping her eyes around the room because she couldn't move her hands. "Maybe that's it, Magadan. Maybe Kohl's in competition with you, and you want him out of the way."

"That's insane! Will you listen to reason?"

"I was willing to listen to reason, and the truth, earlier. It's too late for that now."

Magadan released her and stepped back. His face seemed to have aged. "It can't be too late."

Because she couldn't stand to look at his face, Chela turned away. "Don't worry about that," she said dully. "I made a promise to bring Kohl to justice. I'm not going to go back on my word."

Magadan touched her cheek briefly. "That wasn't what I was talking about."

"I know," Chela whispered and started to grope her way toward the door. She still didn't have the answer she'd come for, but it no longer mattered. Maybe Magadan knew Lou Dye was her father, maybe he didn't. She knew that her life was falling in ruin around her and that was all she had the strength for.

Chela reached the door and had started to turn the knob before Magadan stopped her. "Don't go," he said softly. "We've both said things we regret."

Chela kept her back to him; she didn't dare turn around. "At least we agree on that. It's sad that's the only honest thing that's been said." She wondered if her words hurt him. They couldn't possibly tear him apart as much as they were ruining her. "I don't ever want to see you again," she said. "Do you understand?"

He grabbed her arm and pulled her back around until she had no choice but to show him her wounded eyes. "No, I don't understand that!" he raged. "And I'm not going to live by that insane rule. Chela, we have to talk."

Oh, yes, of course. She'd almost forgotten. "Kohl will be getting in touch with me in a week," she pointed out, keeping her voice emotionless. "We'll talk then."

"No!" He shook her angrily.

"Let me go! You're hurting me!"

Magadan stopped. He backed away from her, his face contorted. "I'm sorry. I didn't mean to. But, damn it, Kohl isn't what I want to talk about."

Chela could only shake her head. She'd done enough talking—and yelling—to last a lifetime. "Not today." She turned back toward the door. "Not ever," she whispered.

This time Magadan let her go. She could hear him breathing even after she'd closed the door between them. The sound of his breath was fresh torture to an already tortured mind.

Why had she wanted to hurt him so much? Whether or not she'd succeeded wasn't the issue. She'd been wrong, cruel, to call him a coyote. Magadan was so far removed from what Kohl was that even in her worst moments she didn't believe that.

But the words had been said; there was no taking them back. Magadan had kept certain things, vital things, from her. That hurt. In turn she'd been determined to hurt him.

But what made the pain in her head almost blinding was the simple fact that she'd been hurt far more than he could ever be.

Chapter Eleven

On Monday Chela boxed up the peach dress and placed it on Magadan's doorstep. When she got home from work the next day, the package was on her doorstep. There was a short note attached to it. "It's yours. It'll always be yours."

Chela removed the dress from its box and held it up to her. Fumbling, she unlocked her door and stumbled inside. She'd lived in a kind of mental and emotional vacuum for two days, but the sight of Magadan's handwriting brought it all back. There was no fighting the memories that went with the dress and what happened after Magadan took it off her in a dark orchard. If only she could go back to that innocent time!

Chela held the dress at arm's length for a long moment and then started to hang it up. Innocence was for babies and children. What she'd been from the moment Magadan entered her life was a fool. Only a fool would be content with the veil of secrecy Magadan wrapped around himself. If she hadn't been dangerously close to tears, she would have laughed at the memory of what she'd been. Yes, she'd been cautious at first, but not cautious enough. What had happened to the instinct that kept her lonely but separate all her life? That was the one essential lesson her mother had tried to teach her before she died. Her true heritage was Mexican. It was insane for her to think she could find happiness with an Anglo.

No more! Chela turned away from the dress hanging limp in her closet. Too many hurting words had been said in Magadan's house the other day. What was almost a joke was that she no longer cared whether Magadan knew who her father was. The chasm that existed between her and Magadan now was too great. It didn't matter whether either of them could see across it.

You're Mexican, Chela told herself. *This is where you belong.* Let Magadan and his kind have their grand homes and vast orchards. Her life was as a migrant teacher, nothing more.

No. That wasn't strictly true. She would have to deal with Magadan until this business with Kohl was over. It was funny in a sad sort of way, but right now Chela didn't care whether Kohl fell into their trap or not. Bringing him to the end of his evil career meant she would have to be clever and determined. Tonight Chela felt neither. She felt empty, wounded, in love, and hating herself for still being in love.

Chela still felt the same way after cleansing herself of the day's dirt and wandering aimlessly through the kitchen for a dinner her body but not her spirit needed. Chela turned on the TV and stared listlessly at it until canned laughter forced her to turn it off. She switched to an FM radio station and tried to lose herself in the music. But it only made her feel like crying.

Chela was almost relieved to hear the knock on her front door. She knew by the sound that it was Magadan's hand, but maybe talking to him was better than having her head fill to bursting with unspent tears.

"We need to talk," he said before the door was fully open.

Chela nodded and stepped back. He was back in his more usual costume of slacks and knit pullover shirt, but he seemed to have lost some of his usual bounce. Chela didn't dare think about that; instead she closed the door. "What do you want to talk about?" she challenged.

"Aren't you going to invite me to sit down?"

"You didn't ask me that when I came to see you. I wasn't clean enough for your furnishings, was I?" she asked bitterly.

Magadan shook his head like a weary bulldog after a battle and sank into his accustomed seat. "Those aren't my furnishings. They belonged to Lou Dye. I haven't had time to do anything with them. You can have them."

"How nice. They aren't anything but castaways, are they? Why not give them to the dirty little Mexican girl?"

"Will you stop that! God! Why didn't I tell you? Why didn't I take my chances then?"

Chela slid into her recliner. But she didn't tuck her feet up under her. She wanted to be able to scurry away should Magadan try to touch her. "Would it have made a difference?" she asked.

"Probably." Magadan reached into his pocket and pulled out a hefty envelope. "I might not be giving you this if I had."

Chela looked at the envelope as he placed it on her coffee table. "Kohl isn't supposed to be getting in touch with me yet," she pointed out, clinging to the hope that their conversation could remain impersonal.

Magadan frowned and ran his fingers through his hair. "I tried to get in touch with Ortez this morning. He isn't there. I think he's on his way here with Kohl."

"Oh, so soon." Chela frowned at the trepidation in her voice.

Magadan leaned forward, studying her. "Have you changed your mind? Maybe you want out of this."

"Don't you think it's a little late for that?" she laughed bitterly. "You must know what he would do if I didn't have his money ready for him."

"I'll kill him if he touches you." Magadan's eyes glowed fiery lights for several heartbeats before relenting. "Look, you're going to have to be very careful. There's no telling what Kohl might do if he smells something."

"He already has, Magadan." Chela laughed her bitter laugh again, thinking of her father's alliance with the coyote and their threat to expose Lou as her father.

"What do you mean?"

It didn't matter anymore, Chela told herself. There was nothing left to try to salvage between her and Magadan. "I mean, Kohl thinks he's done what he needs to to protect himself from me. He doesn't need to resort to violence. Kohl has no reason to doubt that he'll get his money from me." She nodded at the envelope. "All I have to do is hand it over to him."

"Unless he asks for more."

That was a possibility Chela was well aware of. "Then we'll give him more. After all, you're a rich

man," she mocked. "You can come up with whatever
amount he asks for. I just hope you're as good at bringing him to justice as you are at providing money."

"You can't forget it, can you, Chela?" Magadan
asked, the challenge in his voice laced with sadness. "Is
it such a crime to be rich?"

"I never said it was a crime. Forget it, Magadan. We
have nothing to talk about." Chela hated the vindic-
tiveness in her voice, but it was the only defense
against pain she'd been able to find.

Magadan shook his head. "You're wrong about that.
There's one more detail we have to work out. The
method of communication between us when Kohl gets
in touch with you. I want to be there when that happens."

"How? I'm not going to let you stay here. Don't
even suggest it."

"I know, you've made that very clear. But there has
to be a signal, some way of letting me know when Kohl
contacts you."

"I'll call you."

"Not good enough. I don't want you alone here with
him."

Chela knew she wouldn't be alone. Her father would
be there, too. "Whatever happens I can handle it,"
Chela snapped bitterly. "You're not talking to one of
your laborers, Magadan. Don't try to order me around.
I've always been able to take care of myself."

"Maybe it's time that changed. Chela, I'm not going
to walk out that door and leave you to face this alone. I
don't care what you want. I'm getting in touch with the
police, have them keep an eye on you."

"Why? So they can spy on me?"

"Will you stop that! So they can protect you. Look." Magadan fastened his eyes on her, the fire she'd seen before, glowing deep in the dark depths. "You need someone on your side. If you won't have me, then it'll have to be the police."

Chela shrugged, wanting to say things that would hurt him. "Go ahead. Everything we've done has been your way, on your terms. Why should it change now?"

"That's right." Magadan got to his feet, his eyes boring a hole through her. "Why should things change now? They're going to go my way. And when this is over, you and I are going to talk and not stop talking until we have everything straightened out."

"I don't think so, Magadan," Chela retorted with equal determination. "You can't always have the upper hand. There's a limit to your power whether you want to admit it or not. I have to deal with you until Kohl is brought to justice. After that? After that we have nothing in common."

"Nothing?" Before she could draw away Magadan took her hand. He drew her hand up to his chest and placed her palm against the exposure of flesh above the opening in his shirt. "Don't try to lie to yourself, Chela. We shared something once. You can't deny that."

"Can't I?" She tried to pull away, denying her fingers the pleasure of feeling his flesh. "It was all a game with you. You wanted to see if you could fool the ignorant woman from the orchards. Maybe I was doing the same. Maybe I never felt anything for you."

"If I believed that, I wouldn't fight for you." Magadan brought her hand to his mouth, kissed it. "We'll never know if there's anything to salvage if we don't try."

Magadan left then, left his words to echo in the room. Chela's mind was filled with confusion. She had thrown enough hateful words at him to make him regret the day they'd met. What could possibly possess him to talk to a woman who wanted nothing to do with him? That's what she wanted—wasn't it? She wanted to forget his existence. Then why was she crying?

The pain of tears filling her already pounding head was what forced Chela to fight for self-control. She was already half blinded from the headache that hadn't stopped since she confronted Magadan the other day. Her head couldn't stand any more. Slowly Chela pulled herself into a sitting position and took a deep, shuddering breath. Tears weren't for independent women proud of their heritage. They were for weak children who leaned too much on others and depended not enough on themselves.

"Tears, Chela?"

Chela strangled a scream and whirled around. Standing in the doorway to her bedroom was her father. "What are you— Get out of here!"

Lou Dye folded his arms across his chest. His arms found a resting spot on his belly. "I don't think so. I've been waiting down the road, watching you for two days. Now it's going to pay off."

For two days! How much did he know? "Why were you spying on me?" Chela managed as she fought to pull her senses together. "Did Kohl tell you to do that?"

"It's a good thing he did. Can you blame him for not trusting you, daughter?"

Chela rocked to her feet, her hands balling into fists. "Don't call me your daughter! It's too late for that."

"What I call you isn't going to change reality, Chela. Maybe it's something neither of us has been eager to acknowledge, but it is reality."

"It doesn't have anything to do with today. What are you doing here?" Her father looked older than she remembered. The power and arrogance she remembered from a few years ago when she watched him from afar seemed to have slipped. Perhaps bankruptcy had really destroyed him. "What do you want?"

"Answers." Lou came into the room and closed the door behind him. "What was Joe Magadan doing here?"

So he had seen Magadan, Chela acknowledged. "What do you care?"

"Because that man ruined me. He lives in my house now. He's taken what should be mine."

"You lost everything on your own. Your greed caught up with you," Chela snapped back. The thought that her father had closed her in the bedroom bothered Chela, but she wasn't going to order him out, not until she'd learned more. "Don't blame anyone else."

"Is that what Magadan told you? That he was there simply to pick up the pieces, take advantage of my misfortune? Don't believe him." Lou's mouth tightened. "The man will lie about anything, anytime."

"I don't believe you."

"Believe me, daughter." Lou's eyes actually met hers for a moment. "I can understand the power a man like Magadan could wield over a woman like you. He has an intensity some people have mistaken for compassion. But watch him, Chela. He'll bleed you and leave you the way he left me."

Chela clamped her hands over her ears. "What are you talking about? He isn't like that." She couldn't decide why she was defending him. Her father was simply repeating accusations she'd just finished throwing at Magadan herself.

"What do you know? What do you know about deceit and lies?" Lou folded his hands and leaned against the door. "Where do you think I got money for certain loans? From Joe Magadan the businessman. And when I began to have losses, when the orchard failed for two years in a row and I had nothing to send to the canneries, who do you think demanded his money back? Magadan wanted to see me ruined. Joe Magadan wanted all I owned for himself."

"You're lying." Chela's hands over her ears weren't enough. She could hear everything her father was telling her. "Magadan isn't like that."

"Maybe not in bed, but he's a ruthless businessman. He ruined me, Chela. He's responsible for the bankruptcy. I'd still have the orchard if he hadn't come after me. Put your trust in him, and he'll ruin you, too. I—I begged for the time to get back on my feet. I could have gotten another loan so I could improve the orchard, but Magadan saw to it that no one would give me a penny."

Chela refused to think about that. Why should she believe anything her father told her? They had never spent an honest moment together. "Don't talk to me about lies," she spat. "You lied to your workers. You gave them empty promises instead of paychecks. It caught up with you. That's why you lost everything. I've never spent a moment feeling sorry for you."

"Why was Magadan here today?"

Chela blinked. She wasn't ready for the quick switch in conversation. Of course, she couldn't tell her father the truth. He'd tell Kohl and the coyote would bury himself before the law could touch him. Besides, Ortez was with him; that would place Ortez's life in jeopardy. Chela took a calming breath and thought quickly. "Magadan came to tell me I could have some of the furnishings in the house. He said he had no use for them, and Lou's daughter might as well use them."

"Liar!" Lou pushed himself away from the door and brought himself inches away from her. "You're lying to me, Chela."

"I'm not."

"Shut up!" Lou's right hand snaked out and caught Chela on the face. The unexpected blow caused her to lose her balance, and she fell back on the bed. "I want the truth!" Lou screamed.

Chela simply gaped at the man standing over her. Her father had slapped her! The disgust she'd felt for him all those years was a distant thing, nebulous because she never actually came in contact with the man. Now he'd struck her, and all she could think of was the tide of hatred surging through her.

"Let me tell you something, Chela," Lou said when it was clear she was going to remain silent. "Magadan wouldn't be offering you any furnishings because unless you told him, he doesn't know you're my daughter. I never told anyone."

He'd never acknowledged her to a soul. What did it matter? Chela wanted nothing from the man. "He found out," she said in a whisper that lacked the ring of truth.

"You're lying to me." Lou grabbed a length of jet hair and hauled Chela into a sitting position. "There's no way anyone could know we're related. I think maybe that's the only thing we ever saw eye to eye on. Now, what was he doing here?"

Chela's mind whirled frantically within the confines of the trap she'd placed herself in. Magadan didn't know! She scrambled for something to say to her father.

"The money I have for Kohl," she stammered. "It came from Joe Magadan. He—he was taking his payment."

Lou's features underwent a slow but complete transformation. It went from challenging to a look of understanding and—was it resignation? "Why would you go to Magadan for money?" he asked, freeing her hair.

Chela was ready for him. "Who else has that kind of money?" Her head ached where he pulled her hair, and she could feel her cheek stinging, but she refused to touch those spots. "I was desperate. I went to him. He took what I had to offer in the way of payment."

She thought she saw a hint of doubt in Lou's eyes. "So you've become Magadan's lover? He paid for your services?"

Chela recoiled from the trap she'd placed herself in,

but there was no backing down now. She had to protect her true alliance with Magadan. Telling the truth now would endanger Ortez's life. "Magadan doesn't have to pay for any woman's services," Chela said, not understanding why she should be defending the man. "I was the one who came to him. What else was I going to do?" She dropped her eyes in a gesture she hoped signified both embarrassment and defeat.

"Did you know Magadan had ruined me?"

"No!" Chela spat. "How could I? I've never been privy to your dealings. I knew you'd declared bankruptcy, but I knew nothing of the reasons." That was only partly the truth. She would have to be both deaf and blind not to know that Lou Dye was leaving an increasing pile of unpaid debts in his wake. Long before his downfall, she'd expected he'd be exposed.

"That's the way Magadan operates," Lou pointed out. "He does everything under cover of darkness. And now you're caught in his trap. So we have something in common after all, don't we, Chela?"

Her heart denied the accusation, but she kept that emotion to herself. "Are you going to tell Kohl?" The question was a dangerous one to ask, but she had no choice. Her father's answer was essential to the success of the plan to trap the coyote.

Her father appeared to be pondering the question. He stepped backward until he was once again resting his back against the closed bedroom door. Chela remained seated on her bed. She was afraid her legs had lost the strength to hold her. Finally Lou broke the silence. "Not now. I've fulfilled my obligation to Kohl. Why should I help him any more than I have?"

"Thank you," Chela muttered.

"Don't thank me. I'm not doing this out of any feelings for you. I'll never see any of the money you're going to pass on to Kohl. Why should I tell him anything."

Chela was confused. "Then why did you come here with him? Why did you threaten me with exposure?"

In the space of five seconds, Lou's face seemed to age five years. "I have my reasons. Don't cross Kohl. He can destroy you, just as Magadan destroyed me."

Lou turned, opened the bedroom door, and disappeared. Chela waited until she heard the outer door close and then scrambled to lock it. She leaned her hot cheek against the solid wood, trembling from the after-effects of her first true conversation with her father. He wasn't going to tell Kohl that Magadan was involved. That should have filled her with relief, but relief was tempered by some of the other things Lou had said to her.

Not for a moment did Chela believe her father was a helpless pawn trapped by Magadan's greed. Lou had courted his own downfall by cheating his workers and reneging on his contract with the packing house. He hadn't kept up his mortgage and loan payments with several banks. When Lou's little empire came crashing down around him, he had no one to blame but himself.

There was another consideration. It was possible that Magadan had been waiting in the wings, that he had seen Lou Dye teetering at the edge and provided that fatal push. Lou had said he owed Magadan money. It was possible that Magadan had refused to wait for payment and that was what had caused the final collapse.

And if that was the way Magadan operated his business life, maybe it carried over to his personal life as well. Magadan had a deep animosity toward Kohl. For reasons Chela had never fully understood, Magadan wanted the coyote put out of business. Maybe Chela was truly no more than a means to an end.

She didn't want to believe that. God, anything but that! But there was no denying the facts. She had tried several times to tell him she wanted nothing to do with him, but Magadan had kept after her, trading on her sense of outrage of what Kohl stood for, and then cementing their alliance by the promise of something that had been missing from her life.

Chela pushed her weary body away from the door and stumbled into the bathroom. She tried to focus on her swollen cheek, but the pain her father had inflicted was nothing compared to the pain her heart felt.

Secrets! Magadan had had so damn many secrets! She had only one. She refused to acknowledge her father's existence. Was it possible Lou was right, that Magadan didn't know who her father was?

It didn't matter. Magadan had thrown a net over her without having to use her father. He'd offered her warmth and belonging, he'd offered her his body; she'd accepted it all too willingly. Magadan had very nearly gotten away with his deception. If Chela hadn't found out who he was, she might at this moment be lying next to him.

Even the truth hadn't changed things. Chela was still committed to the pact she'd made with Magadan. She doubted he'd care that she'd agreed to meet with Kohl, not because she wanted to work hand in glove with

Magadan, but because the safety of a young Mexican was at stake. For that, bringing Kohl to his knees was worth any cost to her.

Chela would land on her feet. She'd gone through life alone. She knew how to do that simple thing. She had no further need for Joe Magadan.

Then why were tears blurring her reflection in the mirror?

For the next five days Chela drove herself at a killing pace. She doubled her efforts in the orchards to make sure that the new workers coming in for the harvest season knew of the migrant services in the valley. She met several new families and accompanied them to the schools so their children would be registered. It bothered her to know that these children would probably move on once the harvest had been completed, but at least they were assured of a few months of education here. A reporter from the local newspaper came out to interview her, and Chela spent extra time making sure the reporter was aware that migrant education went on both inside and outside the classrooms. She even convinced the reporter to let her add several paragraphs in Spanish in the hopes the article would reach migrants she didn't know about.

The work filled Chela's days, and soccer games filled two more evenings, but there was still too much time left for her to be alone in her house. She longed to slam the door behind her, climb into her Jeep, and drive until she ran out of gas, but she couldn't. She had no idea when Kohl would try to get in touch with her; she had to be accessible to him.

Magadan didn't get in touch with her during that

time, but once, near the start of one of the soccer games, she knew she felt his eyes on her. She didn't want to look around for him, didn't want to give him that satisfaction, but her heart ruled. Chela shaded her eyes against the setting sun and swept her eyes over the boundaries of the city park. It might have been he under a tree near the parking lot, but Chela would never be sure.

So, Magadan had made good on his promise to give her protection, Chela realized one evening when she saw a dark car parked down the road from her house. She tried to tell herself that that was simply a safety precaution a shrewd businessman would take, but her heart continued to hope he was thinking of her and not Kohl's capture when he arranged for a surveillance.

Chela was sleeping restlessly on Friday night. No matter how hard she drove herself during the day, she was unable to sleep through the night without reaching out for something, someone, next to her. When the 4:00 A.M. phone call came, she was almost grateful to be taken from her dream. She groped for the phone near her bed and propped herself up on one elbow.

"You have a half hour to get here with the money," the disembodied voice said. "If you want to see him, I'll expect you at the city park, near the parking lot."

That was it. Kohl hung up before Chela could speak.

She swung out of bed and snapped on the lamp next to the telephone. For an instant she stared at the phone. It was the middle of the night, and she was going to see Kohl—alone.

She wasn't sure why that should terrify her, that was how she'd envisioned it from the beginning. Chela shook her head angrily and quickly threw on an old shirt, an equally old pair of jeans, and slipped her feet into tennis shoes. She tied the laces carefully: If she had to run, she didn't want them tripping her up. She pocketed the money Magadan had given her and stepped outside. It wasn't until she'd reached her Jeep that she realized there was no sign of the car that had been parked on the road for the past few days. Wasn't anyone going to follow her to the park where children played soccer by day and coyotes dealt in human lives by night?

Chela ran back inside and dialed Magadan's number. The phone rang hollowly at least ten times before she gave up. Where was he at this hour? Chela slammed the receiver back down. "Damn you, Magadan! I don't need you!" she hissed at the instrument and hurried back outside.

The night was cool for August, but Chela was sweating instead of shivering as she forced herself to drive within the speed limit. As she drove, she tried to rehearse what she was going to say. Ortez's safety had to be the first consideration. She had to plan her words carefully, do or say nothing that would cause Kohl to be any more suspicious than he already was. It was Ortez's testimony that would guarantee the success of the case. If Ortez had indeed been spirited here under cover of darkness, slipped across the border by Kohl, he would be exposed as a coyote. Nothing could go wrong now. She—and Magadan—had invested too much in this.

Why weren't the police where Magadan said they'd be? True, the case could be built against Kohl at any time, but how much more solid the evidence would be if he was picked up tonight while the transaction was actually taking place. That was supposed to be Magadan's department. Chela only had to play the role of a love-struck woman willing to hock her soul to have an illegal Mexican brought to her by Kohl.

If she hadn't been so tense, Chela would have laughed at the idea of her having to pretend great love for a man she'd never met. She could only hope Ortez was an accomplished actor.

The park, which seemed friendly and filled with life when a soccer game was being played, had turned into a sinister, empty stretch of grass and trees. As she neared the parking lot, Chela could just make out the empty swings swaying under a dim fluorescent light. There were too many shadows and not enough light. The shopping center across the four-lane street, which was the only structure near the park, was empty, a hollow skeleton waiting for the new day to bring it back to life.

Chela pulled into the parking lot and killed her engine. Hers was the only vehicle there, but she still wished her Jeep had a top, something she could lock to protect herself from prying eyes.

Maybe Kohl was already there. It was just like the coyote to use darkness to his advantage so he could observe her while keeping himself hidden. Because that was what she expected him to do, Chela took in a deep gulp of air and swung her body out of her Jeep. She allowed herself an instant to glance down at her tennis shoes. Given the state of her nerves, she didn't think there was a man alive who could catch her should she decide to run.

The knowledge gave her courage. The park had enough open spaces so she could stand in the middle of the grass playing field. No one could sneak up on her. She moved quickly to the grass and stood there until dew began to dampen her shoes. She started at the sound of a distant motor but dismissed it as she saw a lone street sweeper move into the shopping center parking lot. A moment later she glanced back at the street sweeper. Knowing that someone was working this early gave her a small sense of comfort. She wasn't the only one in this part of the city.

Chela heard him. It was nothing more than a foot crushing a fallen twig, but her ignited senses recorded the sound and accepted it for what it was. Tense, she touched the envelope full of money in her back pocket. Where had the police gone?

Kohl wasn't in any hurry to reach her. He seemed to amble along, fascinated by the contours of the park, the size of a swing, the material used to make a backstop. He even took time to test his balance on the pitcher's mound. When he finally came near enough for Chela to make out his features, she could see that he was grinning.

Chapter Twelve

"Where's Ortez?" she asked, when he came into full view.

"Not so fast, my wild one. I'm not fool enough to turn him over until I have my payment."

Chela acknowledged the wisdom of Kohl's words, but she also remembered that she was supposed to be a woman in love. "Where do you have him?" she pressed. "If he's been hurt—"

"What would you do, Chela? What would you do if your precious Ortez was dead? He's an illegal. You couldn't run to the police with that story. You and I are the only ones who know he's here. It would be your word against mine."

Chela spread her feet to balance herself and continued the sparring. "My father knows."

"Your father wouldn't speak against me. I know too much about him."

Chela didn't doubt that for a moment. "What do you want?"

"Money." Kohl stuck out long, skinny, tobacco-stained fingers. "Now."

Chela reached into her back pocket and placed the

envelope in the outstretched hand. "Count it," she challenged. "Then take me to Ortez."

Kohl handled the money as if it were a beloved child. "Not new money. You show wisdom, Chela, but"—he smiled his yellow-toothed smile again—"it isn't enough."

Chela stiffened and clenched her fist, but inside she was calm. She'd expected that. "It's all I have," she said, throwing a slight quaver into her voice.

"Then you won't see Ortez."

"You can't do that to me!" she begged with what she hoped was the right amount of desperation. "You—I already came up with everything I have."

"That was before your lover complicated things." He sounded as if he was trying to explain a simple concept to a child. "The man did things I didn't like. He didn't show me the proper amount of respect."

"What did you do to him?" This time Chela's concern was genuine.

"Nothing that will make him unacceptable as a lover. He had the arrogance to think that because a sizable amount of money was involved, he could expect better treatment."

"What did you do to him?" Chela repeated.

Kohl's lips curled back again. "I taught him respect, just as I will teach you respect. It isn't enough money."

"Wh—what do you want from me?" Chela stammered. Now she was no longer acting. She was fighting for the safety of a man she'd never met.

"Payment for my added trouble."

"I don't have any more."

Kohl took a menacing step toward her. "Get it."

"How?" Chela retreated and spread her hands in a helpless gesture. No matter what other thoughts were going through her mind, she had to remember her agreed-upon role. She had to make Kohl believe he had the upper hand. "There's no way—"

"You came up with a thousand earlier. You can come up with another thousand." His long fingers snaked out and captured Chela's wrist. "You've been a lot of trouble to me for a long time; maybe I should make you pay for that, too."

Chela tried to jerk away, but Kohl's fingers were like iron digging into her wrist. "Let me go!" she snapped, knowing how hollow her order was. "How do I know Ortez is here? I need proof."

"Proof?" He jerked on Chela's wrist until he'd pulled her next to him. "You don't believe me? I'm crushed." His lips were only inches away.

Chela remembered his lips on hers earlier and fought down a gagging reflex. "Why should I?" she managed, despite the whirring sound that started in her head. Careful. She didn't dare lose control now. She had to make him take the money, reveal where Ortez was, and only then when he'd let her go, she'd run to the police. "Why should I believe you?" she challenged in the mocking tone she knew he expected from her. "There's never been any trust between us."

"You challenge me?" Kohl's lips curled again but this time to reveal a snarl. "No one challenges me, Chela."

"Because you only deal with desperate, frightened people," she spat back. "I'm not afraid of you, and I'm not desperate."

"Then you're a fool. You were a fool to come here in the middle of the night to meet me."

Maybe he was right, Chela acknowledged. She had always been able to control her life's direction. Maybe it had lulled her into false security. But she wasn't going to let Kohl know what effect his words had on her. "I don't think so," she challenged again. "Do you really think I'd come here without telling anyone what I was doing? I've left word."

He wrinkled his brow and his fingers dug even deeper into Chela's throbbing wrist. "Who?".

"Do you think I'd tell you that?" Chela sensed the crack in his armor and zeroed in on it. "If I'm not back home by daylight, they'll come looking for you."

"You're lying," Kohl yanked her off balance. "Tell me you're lying!"

"I'm not lying," she gritted, despite having been thrown against him. She used her free hand to push against his chest and regained her balance. "Are you willing to take that chance?"

Before she had time to react, he was dragging her toward his car. She tried to struggle, but her wrist was throbbing, her fingers numb from lack of circulation. It was easier to go with him than to fight. She didn't dig in her heels until he'd reached the car parked in the trees on a bike path where it couldn't be seen from the park. "Where are we going?"

"To take you to your precious Ortez. You can see him, have your tender reunion, and then"—Kohl yanked open the passenger door and shoved her inside—"if you don't want me to make good on my promise to reveal your father's identity, you'll come up with that extra money."

Every instinct Chela possessed aimed at survival was screaming at her to leap from the car and run, but she swallowed the impulse and sat, rubbing her aching wrist while Kohl came around and got in next to her. Her safety wasn't the only thing she had to consider. There was Ortez. What would happen to him if she fled now?

Damn Magadan! Where was he?

As Kohl backed down the bike path, Chela concentrated on breathing. The closed-up car reeked of sweat and stale tobacco and some vile odor that clung to him no matter what new outfit he dressed himself in. She thought about her Jeep in the parking lot. If she never returned, how long would it be before it was identified as hers and before Magadan started to wonder what had become of her?

While Kohl drove through the dark, familiar streets, Chela rubbed her already bruised wrist and glared at him from under cover of her long lashes. She was afraid; there was no denying that. But Chela was also so angry that she could taste the emotion rising in her throat. Whether her anger was directed more at Kohl or Magadan didn't matter. It was enough that she had to fight her fury.

He drove through the downtown area and turned onto the southbound highway that led past used-car lots, second-hand stores, and several run-down trailer parks. After a couple of miles, he turned right and bumped over railroad tracks, ending up on a dirt road that angled behind a large warehouse used by one of the fruit-packing companies during the harvest season. He stopped at the rear of a metal, windowless building in the middle of an unimproved parking lot surrounded by an open field with several boxcars and automobiles rusting in it. "My office," he snickered.

Chela waited for Kohl to turn off the engine and then got out. There was a distant rumble coming from well down the railroad track, but other than that, the area was bathed in silence. Chela felt heat coming from the packed-earth parking lot and acknowledged the swirling wind that blew dust into her face. Above she could see the star-stenciled night. Behind her was the eerie outline of silent storage buildings. She had been born and raised in this valley, but this was the first time she'd come to this lonely, lifeless place.

"You like it?" Kohl taunted. "Go ahead. Scream. No one will hear."

"I'm not going to scream," Chela taunted back, "but I am surprised. I thought a snake lived in the grass, not an abandoned building."

His eyes blazed their hatred, but although his hands had curled into a fist, he didn't strike her. Chela clamped her lips shut. Her outburst showed a dangerous lack of wisdom; she wouldn't let it happen again. "Ortez is here?"

"This is what I call my distribution point," Kohl said almost conversationally. "The workers come here first. From here they're dispersed to wherever they can find work."

Chela almost laughed. What did he think he was, a businessman providing a product for other businessmen? Why not? That was what her father had come to him for. And maybe that's how Magadan used him. "I want to see Ortez."

"In a hurry, Chela? He must be quite the lover to be worth all this trouble. Wait." As she started to move closer to the windowless building, Chela felt Kohl grab her shoulder. "Are you sure you understand the rules? Ortez is yours, but if I don't get my money, I tell him and the rest of the valley about your dear loving father. You know the price of my silence, don't you?"

Chela nodded. A thousand dollars? She'd be a fool if she thought this was all he would want. How many times would the coyote reach out his greedy hand? But that wasn't going to be a problem, not if Magadan made good on his promise. Tonight Kohl was exposing his evil world. The trap was in place. A few more steps and he would be snared.

And if he shrieked the truth about Chela's father?

She had no choice but to live with that. Chela had struck a bargain with Magadan. It was too late to back out now.

Kohl pulled a key out of his hip pocket and freed the lock on the heavy sliding door that made up one side of the storage shed. He leaned his shoulder into the door and pushed it back just far enough to let him and Chela in. Chela blinked repeatedly, but there was no way she could see in the total darkness. She recoiled against the feel of Kohl's hand on her upper arm but had no alternative but to follow his lead. Finally he finished picking his way past boxes and fencing material and tractor parts and reached up. A naked light bulb hanging from a spiderweb-coated cord blinked into feeble life. It was

several seconds before Chela could make out the figure
propped up against a mound of burlap bags.

The figure stirred, stretched, and came to its feet.
"¿Dónde es Chela?"

Chela stared at the man Kohl believed to be her
lover. Ortez was tall, a broad-shouldered man with a
thick shock of black hair, but in the dim light she could
make out little of his features. She felt Kohl's eyes on
her and held out her hands. *"Ortez. ¿Es bien? ¡Me
amante!"*

To Chela's relief she was swallowed by strong arms.
"Me amante," Ortez Varela echoed. *"Por dios."*

"¡Calla! Be quiet!" Kohl snapped. "Enough. Have
you seen enough, Chela? Do you believe me now?"

Chela strangled an insane impulse to laugh. She was
being smothered in kisses by a man she'd never seen
and in turn was cooing over him as if he were her long
lost lover. At least Magadan had been right about that.
Ortez knew his role well. "Are you all right?" she
asked Ortez in Spanish and relaxed a little when he
nodded his head. She didn't put anything past Kohl.

"I want to leave, now—with Ortez," she told him
from the depths of the Mexican's chest.

"How?" Kohl taunted. "Are you going to walk?"

"If we have to. You have your money. What else do
you need?"

"Not so fast, my wild one." He planted himself in
front of the embracing couple. "You've forgotten
something."

"I've forgotten nothing," Chela replied. "I know
what you want."

"In three days. I'll expect you back here in three
days. Otherwise the world knows."

If Ortez was curious about what was taking place, he at least had the wisdom not to ask. He wrapped his arm protectively around Chela and turned her in the direction of the heavy sliding door. "Don't stop us now," he warned Kohl in Spanish.

"I have no intention of stopping you," he returned. He patted the envelope in his back pocket. "I have what I want. Just remember: One word about anything that's happened, and you're back across the border so fast you won't have time to breathe. Or maybe I can arrange to have you thrown into jail. You wouldn't like our American jails. They don't allow conjugal visits."

Chela flushed under the pointed jab, but Ortez was steering her toward the door. He was safe; for the moment they were both safe. All she could handle was one step at a time. *"Calla,"* Ortez whispered. *"Al momento."*

Ortez let her go through the heavy door first. He stood beside her in the dark. "You didn't bring a car?" he asked in English.

Chela shook her head. "That's Kohl's," she whispered, although there was no longer any need. For some reason her legs were shaking. She wondered if she really felt that much relief now that everything was over—or was it over? Where were the police, Magadan? "Are you all right?" she asked. "He didn't hurt you?"

Ortez laughed. "Other than leaving me locked inside that building since yesterday, it hasn't been bad. He doesn't know I speak English. I heard many things he wouldn't want me to know. He'll live to regret that. Are you up to walking?"

"It's better than staying here." A gust of wind hit

Chela's face, but this time instead of closing her eyes against the dust, she fastened her eyes on the dirt road, the distant railroad tracks, the highway beyond. The wind had revived her and reminded her that she was outside. There were no walls holding her. Chela linked her hands with the man whose face she'd yet to see and laughed up at him. "*Me amante*, you're a good actor."

"I'd do almost anything for Joe Magadan," Ortez said as they took their first steps away from what had recently been Ortez's prison.

And I've done all he asked me to do, Chela thought. From now on everything was out of her hands. Her mind still was battering its way against the prison Kohl's threat of exposure had placed her in, but because she could find no way out, she concentrated on finding secure footing on the uneven surface. Weeds grew in clumps along the dirt road, reminding her of how isolated this base of operation was. It had been possible for Kohl to spirit illegals into the valley without the authorities discovering him. She was straining to catch any sound from the shed when the distant rumble she attributed to a train became the unmistakable sound of tires crunching along a gravel road.

Chela stopped and with Ortez moved to one side as first one vehicle and then another approached. The lead car bore the insignia of the county sheriff's department; the other was Magadan's pickup.

For a moment Chela was blinded by headlights, then the lead car eased past her and pulled to a stop next to Kohl's car. Magadan stopped his truck next to the two walkers and got out.

"It's been a long time, Ortez," Magadan said as he shook hands with the Mexican. "Are you all right?"

"I'm tired and hungry," Ortez explained, his left hand still holding Chela's fingers. "Where the hell were you? I was starting to think you weren't going to show up."

Magadan grinned, the gesture sending shock waves through Chela despite her best efforts to ignore him. "We tailed Chela and Kohl here, but we had to wait until you were safely outside. Do you have any idea how hard it is to see anything through binoculars in the middle of the night? We'd probably still be waiting if we hadn't seen you two holding hands. That's how we knew you weren't Kohl."

"You followed me here?" Chela asked, dropping her hand to her side as Ortez released her. "How? No one was at the park."

"That's where you're wrong." Magadan was staring at her with an intensity she couldn't fathom and didn't know how to ignore. "Do you remember a street sweeper in the shopping center? I followed you from your house, got the sweeper operator to get me close enough to see what was happening. Then while the two of you were still talking, I called the sheriff."

"Oh." Magadan had been there all along.

"Would you like to go back inside?" Magadan asked. "I think things might be more interesting in there."

Chela wanted nothing to do with the dark, stuffy storage building, but Magadan seemed to have forgotten how much she hated enclosed spaces. He and Ortez were already walking back to the building. After a moment of indecision, Chela followed them.

The lights from two heavy-duty flashlights had been added to the naked light bulb, taking away much of the storage shed's mystery. Chela was surprised to see that there was a telephone and desk in a far corner of the building. Kohl had called it his office, and he wasn't joking.

Kohl, flanked by two sheriff's deputies, was spewing obscenities, seemingly oblivious of the fact that his hands had been cuffed behind him. When he spotted the trio coming toward him, he threw a few choice words at Chela and then Ortez. His eyes went blank when Magadan stepped up and ordered him to be quiet. "Who the hell are you?"

"You'll find that out soon," Magadan challenged. "You're in enough trouble already. Don't make it worse by talking to Chela that way."

"How do you know her? What the hell is going on?" Kohl's piercing eyes flashed between Chela and Magadan and then fastened on Ortez. "You set me up, didn't you? It was all a set-up."

Ortez grinned. "Your greed set you up," Ortez challenged. "Are you surprised by my English? I went to college in the United States. I'm not going to forget a thing: Not how you got me across the border, not the immigration officer who looked the other way, not the name of the truck driver you paid to get me through California, nothing."

"It isn't going to work! You can't make it stick!"

"You're wrong and you know it," Magadan broke in. "We have enough on you to put you out of business for the rest of your life."

Kohl drew his thin lips back over his yellow teeth.

His eyes continued to bore into his captors', but he said nothing as the officers began a minute search of his office. Instead of joining Magadan and Ortez as they watched the officers, Chela stood alone, her fingers wrapped around her arms. When she was in it before, the building had threatened to close in around her, but that sensation was gone. She tried to tell herself it was the improved lighting and the fact that Kohl couldn't touch her, but one glance at Magadan and she knew she was only fooling herself. It was the man's presence, his strength, that turned confinement into something she could accept. It wasn't the first time that had happened to her. Magadan—he hadn't deserted her, not once, she realized now.

Even when Magadan turned from his study of what the police were pulling out of Kohl's desk and fastened his eyes on her, she didn't drop her gaze. She tried to recall what Magadan had said the last time she'd talked to him. "I'll kill Kohl if he touches you." Were those the words of a man protecting his investment or the words of a man who cared? There was something else he'd said that day. When everything was over, they were going to start talking and not stop until everything had been straightened out between them. Chela was beginning to think she believed that.

An exclamation from one of the deputies distracted Magadan. As he again bent over what they'd found on the desk, Chela went back to her own exploration of the shadowy interior. She wondered how many illegals had been housed in this windowless, airless prison while they waited for Kohl to find work for them. She hoped it was possible that it would never again be a

holding pen. Putting Kohl out of business wasn't an
end to the problem of illegals, but it was a start.

"How do you feel now, Chela? Do you really think
you've won?"

She started at the sound of Kohl's challenge but refused to ignore him. "I wasn't looking for a victory,"
she replied. "I don't see it that way."

"I think you do. Chela Reola coming to me asking
for something? And I believed you. When you told me
you had money, I believed you." He shook his head
angrily. "It wasn't your money, was it? Whose was it?"

"Can't you guess?" Magadan asked.

Kohl turned from Chela to Magadan. The little
man's eyes narrowed. "Who are you? Why would you
give Chela money?"

"You said it yourself." Magadan laughed bitterly.
"To set you up."

"And Chela went along with you?" Despite the taunt
in his voice, Kohl was obviously puzzled. "Chela agreed
to work with an Anglo? She loved Ortez that much?"

"Ortez isn't my lover." What did it matter that Kohl
now knew the truth? Those kinds of secrets were no
longer necessary.

"Not your lover?" Kohl frowned. Finally he ran his
tongue over his yellow teeth. "But a man has gotten to
you, hasn't he? Chela Reola has fallen in love with an
Anglo."

Chela turned her back on his cruel taunts. She wasn't
going to listen to anything else he had to say. She
started toward the door, but Magadan stopped her.
"Don't go," he ordered. "I'll take you home."

I don't want to go anywhere with you, Chela wanted to

say, but Magadan's arm around her stopped the words. For a moment, but only a moment, she let her body lean toward his. There had been so many angry words between them—had they erased the loving nights? Right now Chela couldn't remember what those words had been. "Did you find what you needed?" she asked, because not talking left her with too much room for thinking.

"It's all falling into place," Magadan supplied. "Along with what Ortez is going to be able to testify to, I think we've got enough. You did your part well."

"When can I go home?"

"Do you really want to?" Magadan pulled her into a darkened corner of the building and dropped his voice to a whisper. "I saw what Kohl did to you in the park. Are you all right? I wanted to kill him."

"I'm fine. I told you, I knew what Kohl was capable of." Suddenly the pain of Magadan's secrets came back. "At least I knew what he was like even if I knew nothing about you."

"I'm sorry about that. Please believe me." Magadan still hadn't released her arm. He was massaging her wrist with featherlight sweeps of his fingers. "I'd give anything to be able to start over, be up front from the beginning."

"It's too late for that. You said I wouldn't understand." Chela closed her eyes.

"I believed that," he whispered. "If you'd known I was an orchardist, would you have agreed to work with me?"

Chela shook her head. "Maybe," she relented. "If you'd let me see what kind of a man you are."

"What kind of a man am I?"

"I don't know." *A passionate man, a man like no other I've ever known,* Chela said internally. "I called you a coyote," she said aloud instead. "You took Lou Dye's land."

"Because he was destroying it, because someone had to turn things around. That's not what I want to talk about," he whispered fiercely. "I want to talk about us, but not here."

"Where?" Chela wasn't even sure she wanted this meeting.

Magadan's eyes told her he was deliberating the same question. "Not tonight," he groaned. "There's so much more we have to do here."

Lack of sleep had caught up to her, and suddenly she was so exhausted she could barely stand. "I want to go home," Chela whispered.

Magadan dropped her wrist and wrapped his arm around her shoulder. "I'll take you there as soon as we're done here. Please be patient."

Maybe Chela could have denied him his request if he hadn't put his arm around her, but that strong, warm blanket was her undoing. For the second time tonight she sagged toward him, let him bear the weight of her tired body. Her head pounded and her lungs ached for the clean scent of the air outside, but if she was going to find her way outside, it would have to be with Magadan's help.

As if he knew of her confusion, Magadan steered her toward the lighted area where the activity was centered. Chela lifted her head and focused on the deputies preparing to take Kohl from the shed. At least one thing had come to a satisfactory conclusion tonight. Kohl was going to be brought to justice.

"You had better pray I don't get free," he taunted, the glitter in his eyes just as strong as it had ever been. "Because if I do, you're going to regret the day you were born."

"I don't think that's going to happen," one of the deputies replied. "I've got to hand it to you, you were a thorough businessman. You kept thorough records." He waved one of the folders the police had found. "You'd stand a much better chance if these didn't exist."

For the first time Kohl seemed to note what the deputies had uncovered. The glitter in his eyes darkened, as if his glare could incinerate the damning evidence. His eyes flashed from one captor to the other like a wild coyote sensing the extent of the trap closing down around it.

Magadan's body was there to shield Chela from the full impact of Kohl's glare. "I think you've said enough for now, Kohl," he warned.

Kohl's teeth reminded Chela of a coyote snapping at its bounds. The police might be able to put his body behind bars, but there was no way he could be silenced. "Was it all a lie, Chela? I couldn't have used your father to silence you?"

"Her father?" Magadan asked. "What does he have to do with this?"

"You don't know?" Kohl challenged, while the world buckled and burned red before Chela's eyes.

"Why don't you tell me?"

Chela heard the coyote's teeth snapping down around

her heart. "I was right, after all. Wasn't I, Chela? That would silence you." Kohl turned the full force of his revelation on Magadan. "The wild one's father should be in prison for what he's done. Chela's father is Lou Dye."

Chapter Thirteen

Even before the words were out of Kohl's mouth, Chela was running. She ran without thought or direction, sprinting through the open door and diving gratefully into the darkness. She could hear Magadan behind her, calling, but she didn't slow long enough to turn to see whether he was following her.

Even as her tennis shoes created small puffs of dust in the parking lot, Chela wasn't sure why she was running. The closed-in storage shed, Kohl's eyes transmitting his loathing of her, the sudden tension in Magadan's arm as Kohl's words registered, all confused her and catapulted her into action.

Chela ran lightly, taking minute pleasure in the fact that her slight, athletic body was made for running. The ground around her was flat, which meant there was little danger she would trip and fall in the darkness. Already Magadan's voice was becoming fainter. The night had swallowed her up. Chela ran for another ten or fifteen minutes, thinking of nothing except putting one foot in front of the other, the feel of summer night air on her cheeks, the easy way her lungs adjusted to what she was asking them to do. She didn't know how, but she felt running was a means of cleansing her mind of Kohl's hateful words.

Finally though, Chela became confused by her surroundings and was forced to slow down. She was no longer on any kind of road or parking area. There was nothing but weeds under her shoes, weeds and rocks and mounds of dirt. Chela stopped, balanced on her toes and peered into the night. She could still hear the deep rumble that came from the train tracks and that gave her a sense of direction, but she was somewhere that was untouched by paved streets, buildings, even orchards.

Her pulse was pounding in her head, but her headache was finally leaving her. She breathed rapidly, pulling needed air back into her lungs until they no longer demanded so much of her. Chela almost laughed. She was like a rabbit running from the threat of a pursuing coyote—but the coyote had already been trapped.

She was running from words, then. Only words.

So Magadan and the deputies knew Lou Dye was her father. That was hardly the end of the world, she admitted. The sun would still come up tomorrow. And—why should she care who was with her when Kohl let it all spill out?

Chela glanced down at her dusty tennis shoes, kicked at the clumps of weeds at her feet, and laughed. There wasn't anything to run from, just as there was nothing to go back to. It was fitting that she should be standing in the middle of this nothing stretch of land in darkness, broken only by a few stars, gathering her thoughts about her.

It was still possible that Kohl would make good on his threat to expose her to anyone and everyone who would listen, but she rather doubted that. Telling the newspapers or her employers that Chela Reola's father was ruthless and unfeeling wouldn't save him. He would be better off concentrating on developing a defense for the case against him. He could no longer buy her silence with threats. It wasn't her testimony that would imprison him; it was what was contained in his ledgers and what Ortez would be telling a judge and jury.

Again Chela laughed, a hollow, aching sound that echoed through her cold body. There was no need to hide. Magadan had what he wanted—Kohl in handcuffs.

Chela slowly retraced her footsteps. It was perhaps twenty minutes before she came close enough to the storage shed to make out the lone car still parked in front of the shed. For a moment she toyed with the idea of taking Kohl's car and driving back to the park but decided against it. The car was probably going to be picked up by the sheriff's department. If she touched it, she might be tampering with evidence.

It didn't really matter. Although it was some four or five miles back to the park and her Jeep, Chela didn't mind the prospect of a long walk. She'd walked like this before, when she and Magadan had argued at the Blue Max.

A pink glow was accenting the morning sky by the time Chela reached her Jeep. She breathed deeply as she settled into her seat, acknowledging the warm air signaling another summer day. She was expected at the

migrant education center later that day to select supple-
mentary texts to be used in classrooms, but that would
have to come later. Right now all she could think of
was getting home and climbing into her tub. Maybe, if
she shampooed her hair and scrubbed her face, the
sense of lethargy would leave her.

I'm just tired, Chela tried to tell herself. *I've been up
all night; I saw a man arrested, and I came face to face
with Magadan. I'm having trouble sorting through that,
that's all.*

Even as Chela was trying to convince herself that a
bath was what she needed to restore herself, both body
and soul, she knew it was a lie. Joe Magadan had
touched her life. Even though he was no longer part of
that life, she would never be the same again.

Chela started to back out of the parking lot, caught a
glimpse of the sun rising over the surrounding hills,
and dropped her forehead to the steering wheel. She'd
never share a moment like that with Magadan. For the
rest of her life, she'd have to struggle with the fact that
she'd come close, oh so close, to sharing herself with a
man.

*How do I go back to what I was before I met you, Maga-
dan?* she asked around her tears. *How do I forget what
you did to my heart?* There was no forgetting. There was
only coping.

It was five minutes before Chela had regained
enough self-control to trust herself to drive. Her eyes
ached from the unaccustomed tears, and she still saw
through a film. But she was determined not to cry
again, at least not until she was home.

Chela was vaguely aware that she'd developed blisters on her heels from her walk, but it wasn't until she was in her driveway and getting out of the Jeep that she realized how uncomfortable they had become. She limped to her front door, unlocked it, and stepped inside. She kicked off her shoes and locked the door behind her—she didn't want to be disturbed by anyone—then sat down and studied her heels, grimacing because dirt had gotten into the blisters. She was trying to work up the energy to go into the bathroom when her phone began to ring.

Chela stared dully at the instrument, hating it. Finally, when it had rung a half dozen times, she took it off the hook and hurried into the bathroom. Water began to fill the tub as she pulled off her dirty clothes. Chela eased her tired body into the tub and lay unmoving with her head resting against the lip. The warm water slowly seeped into her, increasing her languor but easing some of the ache in her limbs. If only the bath could do the same for her head. If only she could stop thinking about the telephone and wondering if it had been Magadan on the other end.

Chela stayed in the bathroom for over half an hour. Although it didn't need it, she washed her hair twice and gently scrubbed all the dirt out of her blisters. Finally, when the water turned cool, she stepped out of the tub and wrapped herself in a large terry-cloth towel. She limped into the bedroom and stared dully into her closet. She knew she should go to work—they were expecting her—but she couldn't even decide what to wear.

For a minute Chela didn't think she was going to surrender to the impulse. She'd be able to reach into

the closet without touching the peach dress Magadan
had given her. But her fingers acted with a will of their
own, sliding gently down the silky fabric, lingering at
the soft waistline gathers. Chela snapped her eyes shut
and grabbed at the side of the closet for support. She
swayed, feeling light-headed and dangerously close to
tears again. Why did that dress have to be there?

In desperation Chela reached out again and grabbed
the first garment she touched. It was the white eyelet
sun dress she'd worn when she went to Phillip's house
to meet with Magadan. Chela almost dropped the sun
dress but somehow found the courage to hold on to it.
Memories would be part of her for the rest of her life.
Today was soon enough to start dealing with that reality.

Chela slipped into the dress, towel dried her hair,
and limped to the small bathroom mirror. Her eyes
were red-rimmed and dull, but she was beyond caring
about her appearance. No matter how tired she was,
how much her blisters throbbed, she was grateful she
had to get dressed and go to work this morning. It gave
her an excuse to get out of the house and away from
the telephone. Enough things had to be done today to
keep her moving and on her feet until she could fall
into bed exhausted.

Chela poured herself a glass of orange juice and
drank it, but her stomach recoiled at the thought of
food. Her last act before leaving the house was to slip
into a pair of heelless sandals. As she closed the front
door behind her, Chela was thinking about the phone
lying off its hook.

She didn't notice the figure waiting in her Jeep until

it was too late. She was more than halfway between it and the house when she stopped, her body instantly tensed for flight.

"Don't run, Chela. Please. We have to talk."

She stood where she was, unable to think of anything except her throbbing heels. "I have to go to work," she said lamely.

"Not as much as we have to talk. Don't put me off. It has to happen sooner or later."

"No, it doesn't," she responded dully, the effect of her sleepless night and empty stomach weighing her down. "There isn't anything left to say, Magadan."

The man eased his body out of her Jeep but didn't come any closer. He was staring at her figure with an intensity that was nearly her undoing. "Why are you wearing that dress?"

Chela didn't feel strong enough to explain the rationale that had gone into that decision. "It's hot. The dress is cool. Magadan, I have to get to work."

"To hell with work! I'm sorry," Magadan muttered, rubbing a big hand over his eyes. "We've both been through the wringer in the past few hours. I know how tired I am. It has to be even worse for you."

For some inexplicable reason Chela giggled. "I have blisters. That didn't happen the last time I had to walk."

A tentative smile touched Magadan's lips. "You can laugh. That's good. Why did you run away from me last night?"

Chela's urge to laugh died as quickly as it had been born. She shifted her weight, aware of how many hours she'd spent on her feet since she'd last slept. "I don't think you really need to ask me that," she pointed out in clipped tones because she was fighting for self-control. "You know what Kohl said."

"I tried calling you earlier," Magadan said.

"I know. I took the phone off the hook."

The tentative smile touched his lips again. "I'm beat. I know you are, too. Can't we go somewhere where we can at least sit down?"

"I have to go to work."

"The hell you do!" Magadan's long, powerful legs ate up the distance between them. He took her hands in his, not touching the bruised right wrist that bore the marks of Kohl's anger. "Unless you want me to follow you wherever you go today, you'd better agree to this conversation. I'm not going to walk out of your life, Chela."

Chela shook her head but didn't fight him. "We don't live in the same world, Magadan."

"I don't ever want to hear you say that again," he spat. "The only thing that matters is how we feel about each other, not our backgrounds. And we'll never know how we feel if we don't talk."

Maybe Magadan was right. Chela still wanted to turn her back on this intense man, give herself space, and rest, and thinking time. But what good would her thinking do? Would that decide anything? "We should have talked a long time ago," she said, knowing her words could cut and injure but needing to say them anyway. "If only you'd been honest—"

Instead of replying, Magadan pushed her ahead of him until they were at the side of the road where his pickup was parked. "You want honesty?" he asked bitterly as he opened the passenger door and helped her step up into it. "I'll give you honesty."

Chela stared at Magadan as he got in next to her and put the key in the ignition. "Where are we going?" she asked tentatively, tension clipping off the ends of her words. Talking to Magadan about the twists and turns in their relationship could spell the end to everything. But maybe it was over already, and all that remained was the burial.

"To my house."

Chela shivered. "I don't want to go there," she said, surprised at the frightened tone that had broken through her defenses.

Magadan touched her cheek before turning back to the task of driving. "I understand," he said softly, "but I have my reasons. Please trust me."

Trust was a strange word coming from a man who had never trusted her enough to reveal anything of himself. It would be much easier to order him to stop now, to get out of his truck and tell him that nothing existed between them anymore, but a glance at Magadan's profile filled Chela with proof that her heart was a long way from believing that. She had always prided herself on her courage. She wanted Magadan to see that, if nothing else. They traveled in silence until they reached the east hills.

"I wouldn't have chosen this location if it had been up to me," Magadan said conversationally but without looking at Chela. "I was in a hurry to find a place to live, and your father's house was available. The people here have cut themselves off from the rest of the valley. They live in their own closed-in community, safely insulated from certain realities."

Chela looked at Magadan. This time her glance lasted longer than it had when they left her house. "It's where the people with money in the valley come to live," she said.

"Not me. I have little personal use for money. I'm too busy to think about where I hang my hat, how many rooms a house has. There are more important things in life."

"Like what?"

"Like getting rid of men like Kohl. He's been formally charged with things ranging from illegal transporting of migrants to fraud. He may even be charged with kidnapping Ortez. I wanted you to know that. The DA believes the charges are going to stick. There's even evidence he blackmailed some orchardists. The DA hopes he can get them to step forward."

"Will I have to testify?"

"I don't know." Magadan touched her cheek again before pulling into his driveway. "I hope not. Kohl might still make good on his threat."

Chela slumped in her seat and closed her eyes. "It doesn't matter. I don't care anymore."

"I think you do," Magadan objected before coming around to let her out. "I think you care a lot more than you're willing to let on. I hope I can change some of that for you."

"You think you can change my relationship with my father?" Chela asked bitterly. "I never wanted anyone to know who he was." She closed her eyes again, fighting a desire to lean against Magadan. "Least of all you," she managed, her words barely audible.

"Why?" Magadan had started to unlock the front door, but now he stopped.

"I don't know!" Chela hissed. "Why should it matter? You know all about what drives men to take and take and take in order to achieve their end," she said in a bitter tone.

Magadan grabbed Chela's forearm and led her into the house. His blazing eyes boring down on her were echoed by the sound of the door slamming. "What the hell do you mean by that?"

Chela would not cower before him. If he wanted a talk, it would begin. "My father told me."

"Your father told you what?" Magadan asked as he released her.

Chela sank into the recesses of the recliner, and, shaking off the need to relax, began, her words tumbling out almost as if they existed beyond her control. "My father told me how determined you were to get hold of his land, this house. He told me you demanded repayment on the loan you'd given him. He couldn't come up with the money, and when you sued, it broke him."

"He said that?" Magadan hadn't sat down. Instead he was leaning against the wall nearest Chela's recliner. He lifted one leg and planted his shoe against the wall, oblivious of the marks he was leaving on the white surface. "Lou told you I sued him?"

"Yes. Or words to that effect," she faltered slightly. Did she believe anything she was saying? "I didn't understand it all; I've never been part of my father's world. How could I know everything about his business dealings?''

"But you believed him when he blamed me for his downfall?''

Chela returned Magadan's glare. To do otherwise would be to surrender her will to his. "Yes, he had no reason to lie to me.''

"And what if I told you I didn't meet your father until I heard he'd declared bankruptcy. What reason would *I* have to lie to you?''

Chela blinked. What was Magadan saying? He would have to have some contact with her father in order for Lou to borrow from him. Either her father or Magadan had lied to her. "Are you telling me you never had any business dealings with my father?'' she asked, stalling for time while her mind sought a way out of the emotions bombarding her.

"I've seen him once—when we met to sign the necessary papers. I assumed his debts, that's all. What about now, Chela? Which of us are you going to believe?''

"I don't know,'' she moaned. But that wasn't the truth. She had no reason to believe her father, there'd never been any trust, any openness between them. She'd known that so long that the knowledge carried no pain with it. "Is that why you brought me here—to talk about my father?''

"That was one of the things.'' Magadan pushed himself away from the wall and finally settled himself in a couch. Although a coffee table stood between them, Chela felt anything but safe. His eyes, which never left hers, were chains linking them together. "I need to know how you feel about him. I hope you trust me enough to be honest about that.''

"We're talking about us, not my father. I want to know why you wouldn't tell me anything about yourself, why I had to find out about you and this house and Hidden Valley Orchard on my own." Chela kicked off her sandals and tucked her feet up under her white sun dress. She wanted to lock her arms around her knees, but that would tell Magadan too much about the turmoil she was in.

Magadan gave an angry snort. "Do you remember what you were like when you found out? You were half crazy when I saw you sitting on my front step that afternoon. You accused me of a lot of things, of being a coyote. You said I was the kind of man who looked for weakness in people and twisted that around to my advantage."

"I remember," Chela whispered. There were a lot of things she shouldn't have said that day. "But you have to understand I've devoted my life to improving the lives of migrants. I've seen what orchardists can do to make sure those lives don't change. Magadan, my mother owed her soul to an orchardist—it wasn't my father—but she had to borrow money from the orchardist to support us until the harvest came in. She was in his debt. The debt grew and grew until there was no way out. Magadan, he owned her. When I learned you were one of them—"

"You decided to hate me. You don't see it, do you, Chela? You still don't see why I didn't want to tell you who I was.

"I did a lot more than talk to your boss and the sheriff before I contacted you. From my foreman I learned about the old system of putting a laborer in an orchardist's debt. It was a form of slavery. Pedro knew your mother. He told me she was trapped in the orchard. I understand how deep your hatred of orchardists was."

Chela closed her eyes in agony. "You didn't think I could take honesty from you because of that?"

"Do you blame me?"

"I don't know." Chela tried to breathe, but it hurt too much. "Why did she have to die?" she sobbed. "She was all I had in the world."

"Maybe, maybe not. I found something this morning." Magadan surged to his feet and held his hands out toward her. "Come on, you need to see this."

"See what?" Chela pushed her back farther into the recliner, trying to escape the impact of Magadan's eyes.

"Come." He took her arms, pulling her out of the recliner as if she weighed no more than a kitten. "You want honesty? I think I can give you that now."

Chela struggled in his grip, but he didn't seem to notice. He pushed her ahead of him until they reached the flight of stairs leading to the second floor. Chela stumbled twice as Magadan propelled her up the stairs. "When you ran away from me out there, I thought everything was finished between us," he was saying. "I saw the pain in your eyes. You looked so damn alone."

Chela tried to turn around. "You don't have to—"

"The hell I don't."

"Then why didn't you tell me last night?"

Magadan steered her into a room at the top of the stairs. "You weren't in any mood to listen. You were hurting and you needed to be alone at that moment."

He forced her to look into his eyes. "Do you know what I did when I got back here this morning? I started to tear into this room—your father's bedroom. I wanted everything that was his out of here. I didn't get far, because I found something you need to see."

"I don't understand" were the only words Chela could manage to form.

"You will in a minute." Magadan released her while he strode across the room. Chela looked quickly around, trying to take in as much as possible of a magnificent master bedroom dominated by a king-size bed. The windows were covered by heavy brocade draperies. A glass-top mahogany dresser with a huge mirror reflected Chela's startled, wary eyes.

She was still trying to comprehend what she was learning about her father when Magadan shoved a small jewelry box in her hand. "I found this in the back of one of the closets. Your father didn't take anything except his clothes from the house. That was part of the legal agreement. "Go on," he challenged. "Open it."

Chela turned stricken eyes on Magadan, but he was giving her no way out. Slowly, feeling as if she were opening Pandora's box, Chela unfastened the lid and lifted it. Inside were a few newspaper clippings, a faded picture.

She lifted the picture in trembling fingers. It was a black-and-white snapshot of a beautiful Mexican woman holding the hand of a young girl. Chela sobbed as she clasped the picture to her breast and collapsed on the bed. She dropped her head, her heart going back more than twenty years. "That's my mother," she whispered.

"And you're the little girl. Think about that, Chela. Your father kept that picture all those years."

Chela couldn't trust herself to speak; instead she unfolded one of the newspaper clippings and started to read. It was a story written when she'd started going into the orchards to teach the migrants. The story contained a photograph of her surrounded by Mexicans. Her father had underlined her name in the picture caption. The other newspaper clippings were of the same kind. There was one on the migrant education program with a paragraph devoted to her role in it. Another article dealt with her activities in getting the county gleaning project under way. There was even a yellowed column listing her name along with the others graduating from college.

Chela let the papers slip from her fingers. She stared up at Magadan, her mouth open, but nothing came out. She swallowed and tried again. "I never knew."

"There's more to the man than you thought."

"Magadan?" Chela's head was filling with a roaring sound, but she struggled to speak over the rushing tide. "My father came to see me the other day. He—he said he wouldn't let Kohl do anything to me. I didn't understand then. I—I've hated him so long, I believed he felt the same way." She touched the box beside her on the bed but lacked the strength to pick it up. "I was wrong."

Her revelation was the final blow. Tears that had been bottled up inside for years, tears she didn't know she possessed, burst free and overwhelmed her. Chela sagged forward and might have collapsed if Magadan hadn't taken her in his arms.

He held her, rocked her, for long minutes as years of loneliness and a night without sleep combined to hold her helpless in the grip of tears. Magadan was whispering words that had to do with his understanding, but it was the sound and not the words that reached Chela. From the moment of her mother's death, she had never had anyone to put their arms around her. She'd survived without that special brand of love and learned to function. But today, with Magadan to make her world right again, she realized how much it had cost her to carve the strength and independence that went into her being.

"Do you understand?" Magadan whispered. "Do you understand why you had to see this? Chela, darling, your father had some feelings for you."

Darling? He had called her darling. No one had ever done that. "I understand now."

"I hope so." His voice held a trembling note, as if some of her emotions had spilled over to him. "But that isn't enough. You deserve someone in your life now, not memories and faded pictures."

Chela shook her head. She still needed Magadan's arms around her, but she was starting to regain some self-control. Her memories of her mother were precious; her father had some feelings for her after all. The thought warmed her and gave her the courage to speak. "I didn't trust you enough," she managed. "I was afraid to tell you about my father. I—I sensed something good about you, but I didn't want to risk losing you."

"That would never happen," he said, burying his face in her hair, still rocking her trembling body. "I'd never leave you, Chela."

"I—I don't know. I didn't know enough about trusting people."

Gently Magadan pushed her away from his chest and helped her sit erectly. "That's what I'm here for, darling. To show you how to trust me. And to learn to trust my instincts about you. I should have told you everything from the beginning. I kept telling myself that, but I was afraid to risk it. Can you understand that?"

Could she understand experiencing the fragile birth of love and being terrified of watching its death, being a part of what might be called murder? "Yes," she whispered, offering him her lips. "I don't want to be alone anymore."

"Neither do I," he replied, covering her lips with his. "Neither do I."

"Joe?" she managed. "Joe, I love you."

"You called me Joe, not Magadan. Do you mean it?"

"Yes." It was time for the final barrier to fall. "Yes, Joe."

"I love you, Chela."

They didn't leave the bedroom until it was too late for either of them to go to work.

One to Another

A year's supply of Silhouette Desire® novels— absolutely FREE!

Would you like to win a year's supply of seductive and breathtaking romances? Well, you can and they're FREE! Simply complete the missing word competition below and send it to us by 31st January 1997. The first 5 correct entries picked after the closing date will win a year's supply of Silhouette Desire novels (six books every month—worth over £160). What could be easier?

PAPER	**B A C K**	WARDS
ARM		MAN
PAIN		ON
SHOE		TOP
FIRE		MAT
WAIST		HANGER
BED		BOX
BACK		AGE
RAIN		FALL
CHOPPING		ROOM

Please turn over for details of how to enter ☞

How to enter...

There are ten missing words in our grid overleaf.
Each of the missing words must connect up with the
words on either side to make a new word—e.g.
PAPER-BACK-WARDS. As you find each one, write it in
the space provided, we've done the first one for you!

When you have found all the words, don't forget to fill in
your name and address in the space provided below and
pop this page into an envelope (you don't even need a
stamp) and post it today. Hurry—competition ends
31st January 1997.

Silhouette® One to Another
FREEPOST
Croydon
Surrey
CR9 3WZ

Are you a Reader Service Subscriber?   Yes ❑   No ❑

Ms/Mrs/Miss/Mr _____

Address _____

_____

_____ Postcode _____

One application per household.

You may be mailed with other offers from other reputable companies as a
result of this application. If you would prefer not to receive such offers,
please tick box.   ❑

C296
A